ANNA *and the* CAT LADY

by Barbara M. Joosse
pictures by Gretchen Will Mayo

📖 HarperCollins*Publishers*

Anna and the Cat Lady
Text copyright © 1992 by Barbara M. Joosse
Illustrations copyright © 1992 by Gretchen Will Mayo
All rights reserved. No part of this book may be used or
reproduced in any manner whatsoever without written
permission except in the case of brief quotations embodied
in critical articles and reviews. Printed in the United States
of America. For information address HarperCollins
Children's Books, a division of HarperCollins Publishers,
10 East 53rd Street, New York, NY 10022.

Typography by Anahid Hamparian

1   2   3   4   5   6   7   8   9   10
First Edition

Library of Congress Cataloging-in-Publication Data
Joosse, Barbara M.
    Anna and the cat lady / by Barbara Joosse ; pictures by
Gretchen Will Mayo.
        p.   cm.
    Summary: When nine-year-old Anna rescues a stray
kitten, it leads her into friendship with Mrs. Sarafiny, an
eccentric old woman with many cats and a paranoid
conviction that the Martians are after her.
    ISBN 0-06-020242-4. — ISBN 0-06-020243-2 (lib. bdg.)
    [1. Cats—Fiction.   2. Mental illness—Fiction.]
I. Mayo, Gretchen, ill.   II. Title.
PZ7.J7435A1   1992   91-12510
[Fic]—dc20   CIP
                                                 AC

For Don, my brother

Contents

1

THE HAUNTED HOUSE

Anna stretched out her toes and wriggled them against the tips of her too-small sneakers. She touched her hand to the cool glass of the school-bus window. Then Anna reached over to squeeze the hand of her own very best friend, Bethie. Anna sighed. There had been many wonderful days in Anna's life, but this was going to be the best.

"What are you thinking about, Anna?" Bethie asked.

Anna smiled mysteriously. "Today's adventure."

Bethie's root-beer-colored eyes fastened on Anna's chocolate-colored ones. "Tell," she said.

Anna tried to wipe off her smile. She wanted Bethie to get in a mysterious mood, and a smile was the wrong sort of atmosphere. Still, the smile kept tugging at the corners of her mouth, and Anna had to squeeze her lips together with her hand.

"Bethie, you know I can't tell you the adventure—that's an Adventure Club rule. But I will say this: It involves the spirit world."

Bethie sucked a breath in. "Ghosts? Tell me, Anna! Come on! I'm dying to know." Bethie's eyes were saucery-round.

"No, Bethie. It will be more fun if it's a surprise. I'll tell you at the meeting."

The bus slowed down and stopped at the familiar brick house with all the bicycles in front. "Here's your house," Anna said.

Bethie and two of her brothers, Seth and Tom, got off the bus. "See you soon," Bethie yelled through the bus window.

Anna leaned back against her seat. The autumn sky above Egg Harbor was a brilliant blue. Sunshine seemed to fill each corner of Anna's world with glowing light. The trees were fiery colors—reds, golds, and oranges—and it made Anna happy just to look at them. Anna felt as if the inside of her were simmering, like water just before it boils. She hoped when she was very old that she would remember everything about today, the best day of her life.

Anna glanced behind her at her big sister, Kimberly. Kimberly dressed and acted as if she were Princess of the World. Her long, blond hair glinted in the autumn sun. Kimberly's hand lingered on the top of the seat, showing off her Peach Passion nail polish. Anna knew Kimberly placed her hand there on purpose. She wanted everyone to notice her manicured nails. Anna was not allowed to wear polish, and she bit her nails instead of filing them.

The bus stopped at their house on Prairie View Court. Kimberly walked quickly down the aisle, her skirt brushing Anna's arm as she passed. Anna lagged behind and walked down the bus steps very slowly. She did that because it made Kimberly angry when she was so slow. She also did it because she felt important when the bus driver made traffic stop for her. She wanted to make that feeling last as long as she could.

"Anna!" Kimberly said. "Hurry up."

"I am," Anna said.

Kimberly tapped her foot with impatience. "Come on," she said.

But Anna would not let Kimberly hurry her, not today. She walked down the stairs as slowly as she wanted.

"Kimberly," Anna said, "I think you should wear a different color nail polish."

"Why?" Kimberly asked, her blue eyes wide.

"Because . . . actually, that peach stuff looks a little spoiled. Like rotten fruit."

"Oh," Kimberly said, glancing nervously at her manicured nails.

Anna heard the sound of Mrs. Sarafiny's heels tapping the pavement before she saw her round the corner. Then Anna saw the little parade—six cats on leashes and Mrs. Sarafiny. Anna had been curious about this little group ever since she had moved to Egg Harbor. Only recently, she'd begun to pet the kitties as they scampered by and to say "hello" to their cheery owner.

"Hi, Mrs. Sarafiny," Anna called out.

Mrs. Sarafiny nodded hello and continued on

4

her way. Mrs. Sarafiny was short and squishy. She reminded Anna of a jelly-filled doughnut. She was wearing a raspberry-red coat and a funny, floppy-brimmed hat. The hair that stuck out of Mrs. Sarafiny's hat was white and fuzzy like the woolly hair on a rag doll. She wore white, summery shoes and carried a big straw bag with Manzanillo written on it in orange yarn.

Anna felt Mrs. Sarafiny had a perfect life. Anna had always wanted a kitten of her own, but Kimberly was allergic. So Anna had none. And here was Mrs. Sarafiny with not one but six cats! How lucky could you get?

After Mrs. Sarafiny crossed the street, she called over her shoulder. "How do you like my hat?"

"I like it," Anna said.

Mrs. Sarafiny grinned. "I crocheted it myself. It's made out of bread wrappers!"

Sure enough. Mrs. Sarafiny's floppy, shiny hat really was made out of plastic bread wrappers. Anna recognized the familiar blue and white colors of her favorite bread. Anna liked the idea of making your own clothes. She had fashioned many herself. Once she'd made earrings out of frizzed-out yarn and blue jay feathers. Once she'd stapled pop tops onto her blue-jean jacket.

Anna watched Mrs. Sarafiny continue on her way. The cats' leashes were kind of a tangled mess because the cats kept weaving in and out. But somehow the little group continued on. When they were nearly out of sight, Kimberly whispered, "Anna! You shouldn't talk to Mrs. Sarafiny!"

"Why not?" Anna asked.

"Because she's kind of weird."

"I'm weird," Anna said.

Kimberly thought for a while before she answered. "Anna, I admit you aren't a typical third grader. But it's not the same as Mrs. Sarafiny."

"What's wrong with Mrs. Sarafiny?"

"She doesn't dress normally, for one thing," Kimberly said. "She wears summery clothes in cold weather, and that red coat no matter what."

"So?"

"So, it's just not *normal*, that's all." Kimberly shifted her backpack to a more comfortable spot on her shoulder. Anna could tell Kimberly was getting ready for a big speech. Anna sighed. It was bad enough that Daddy liked to give lectury talks. He was an editor, after all, and Anna figured that was part of his job. But now Kimberly had begun to give long speeches like Daddy.

Kimberly's feet were planted firmly on the sidewalk. Her blond hair shone brilliantly in the sun and looked way too much like a holy person's halo to suit Anna. Kimberly continued. "Anna, something is strange about Mrs. Sarafiny. I can't put my finger on it, exactly, but she's"— Kimberly's hands swept the air around her, searching for just the right word—"different. It's like she's a jigsaw puzzle and one piece is missing. Or maybe that she has one piece too many. Take the cats, for example."

"Yes?" Anna said, thinking that's exactly what she'd like to do. In fact, it's exactly what she *would* do if it weren't for Kimberly and her dumb allergies.

"A normal person has one cat. Maybe two. But six? I'm telling you, Anna, you can never tell about Mrs. Sarafiny." Kimberly pointed a finger into the air. "She's *unpredictable*! That's it. Unpredictable."

And that, thought Anna, is exactly what I like about her. But Anna knew better than to say that to Kimberly.

Kimberly walked to the front door, but Anna beat her to it. Inside, Anna flung her backpack to the floor of the closet and threw her jacket toward the hook. Then she ran upstairs to change. She left her school clothes on the bed—she would put them away later—and picked up her jeans and sweatshirt from the floor. It was an Adventure Club rule that you had to wear jeans and a sweatshirt. It was the best outfit for an adventure.

Anna ran back downstairs to write a note for Mom and Daddy. Mom was working at the bookmobile and Daddy was working at the newspaper, the *Door County Advocate*. They wouldn't be home for at least an hour, and by then Anna would be having her adventure. Anna thought, Today's adventure is going to be pretty scary. Even a sixth grader like Kimberly would be frightened to do it. But I will have Bethie and Bethie will have me, so it won't be dangerous. Still, Anna wrote:

Mom and Daddy,

    Bethie and I are having an adventure. I'll probably be back by supper. No matter what, remember that I love you.

        Your daughter,
        Anna

Then Anna grabbed her jacket from the closet floor, let the front door slam behind her, and ran all the way to the Hendersons' farm.

The Adventure Club usually met inside the cow tunnel at the Hendersons' farm. Anna had never seen a cow tunnel in Rockford, Illinois, but here in Door County there were several. Cow tunnels were big cement tubes. They passed under a highway so the cows could move from one pasture to another without going into traffic. The ground on either side of the Hendersons' tunnel was heavily grooved from the cows' hooves. You had to step carefully because of the grooves—and because of the cow pies. But inside the tunnel it was wonderful. It was big enough to stand up in, and because it was round and made of cement, it echoed.

Bethie was waiting inside the tunnel. "Anna!

Hurry up! Tell me about your idea!" Bethie's voice echoed from in there, and it sounded far away and spooky. Spooky was just right for today.

Anna entered the tunnel. She stretched her lips into a thin, serious line. She let her eyebrows pinch together. When Anna crouched down low, she felt the cold from the dirt and cement creep into her skin. Suddenly Anna became nervous. Maybe the cold she felt was not from the dirt and cement. Maybe it was a ghostly warning.

Bethie crouched down too, and Anna began to whisper, "Once there was a man, Charles Streff, who loved a woman more than anything else in the world. The woman's name was Melea. She was beautiful, as beautiful as a flower." Anna searched for just the right words. "As beautiful as Miss Crystal."

"Oh!" Bethie said, convinced.

"Well, Charles loved Melea, but she did not love him back."

"Unrequited love," Bethie said, rocking back on her heels. Bethie's mother read romance novels, so she knew about such things.

"So Charles tried to win Melea's affection. Charles bought Melea many expensive things—

jewelry, a fine horse and carriage, music boxes. Still Melea didn't love him. So Charles built an expensive house for her and bought beautiful furniture to go in it." Anna bent closer. "He even furnished a tiny nursery, ready for a baby they would have one day. Still, Melea didn't love Charles. She wouldn't marry him."

Bethie said, "Then what?"

"Charles became very sad. He grew pale and thin. He sat on his porch swing night after night, waiting for Melea to come."

"But she never came," Bethie said.

"Right."

"And Charles?" asked Bethie.

"He died," Anna said.

Bethie sighed. "Of a broken heart?" she asked.

Anna nodded solemnly.

"Are we going to visit his grave?" asked Bethie.

Anna shook her head. "No." She leaned closer to Bethie. "We're going to visit his house."

"Who lives there now?" Bethie asked.

"No one. The house is empty. In the beginning, after Charles's death, a young family lived there. But they said the place was haunted and they left. No one has lived there since."

Bethie stood up, her hands on her hips, her eyes narrowed and suspicious. "Anna, how did you find out about this house? I never heard about it. Is it really true?"

Anna held up her right hand. "Swear to die! Daddy's doing a series on Wisconsin hauntings for his newspaper. The story of Charles Streff is going to be published just before Halloween. He told me about it."

Anna and Bethie sat very still for several minutes. They were worried about Charles's ghost. How would he feel about two girls snooping around? What would he do about it? But an adventurer must take risks to find out the truth, so that was what they had to do.

Anna and Bethie lingered at the edge of the tunnel. They watched the cows peacefully chewing grass, completely unaware of the adventure that was about to take place. "Let's go," Anna said suddenly.

"Okay."

Anna walked quickly, swinging her arms at her sides, telling herself that absolutely nothing bad would happen. Anna was glad the day was still sunny. She was glad it would be light when they explored the house.

When Anna and Bethie walked to the top of a steep hill and turned a sharp corner, they saw the house. It was very tall and narrow, and it loomed dark against the blue sky. The siding had been weathered to a silvery gray. Most of the windows and the doors on the old house had been boarded up. There were several lightning rods on the tin roof and a creaky weather vane. There were some old, twisty apple trees in the front yard, and a lot of apples lay beneath them. As Anna got closer, she breathed in the sweet apple smell.

Bethie poked Anna with her elbow. "Anna!" she whispered, "the porch swing!" On the porch was a long, carved swing, and it was rocking. That must be where Charles used to sit to wait for Melea! Was the wind making it rock now, or was it something else?

Anna and Bethie walked toward the house. "Are you afraid, Anna?" asked Bethie.

"A little." Anna's heart was banging against her ribs. Her face was pale, and she felt sweaty and cold at the same time. Anna and Bethie circled the house, parting dark, overgrown bushes to look for a way to get inside. They tried the old cellar door but it was padlocked. It was beginning to get dark when Bethie yelled, "Over here, Anna. I think we can get in here!"

Anna rushed over to Bethie. There, on the second floor, was a broken window. It must have been broken a long time, because now it was completely open—there were no pieces of glass remaining. There was a tall tree next to the house. They could climb the tree and get in through the window. But Anna had fallen from a tree once, and she didn't feel she had very good luck with them. Also, Anna had not imagined entering the house this way. She had imagined the sun shining cheerfully, and now it was getting dark. She had imagined walking through a wide doorway and letting the outside air blow in before her. Slithering into a narrow opening on the second floor—feetfirst—was not the way Anna wanted to enter the house and meet whatever waited inside. But there was no other way!

"Should we do 'eenie meenie minie moe' to see who goes first?" asked Anna.

Bethie frowned at Anna. "With two people you

can make 'eenie meenie minie moe' turn out however you want. If you end at 'moe,' you end up pointing at yourself. If you end at 'Y-O-U spells You,' then you end up pointing to the other person. No, Anna, we have to flip a coin or something."

While Anna and Bethie argued, it had become darker still, and now the sun had crept behind a cloud. Anna slid a nickel from her pocket. "You call," she said to Bethie.

"If I win the flip then you go first."

"Okay," Anna agreed. Anna flipped the coin high into the air.

Bethie yelled, "Tails!" but Anna dropped the coin and had to search for it in the overgrown grass. She found it and tried again. "Tails!" yelled Bethie.

Anna caught the coin this time and flipped it over to the back of her hand. Then she looked. It was tails.

2

INSIDE THE HOUSE

Bethie gave Anna a boost to the first branch of the tree. Anna pulled herself up and reached down to help Bethie. Slowly, carefully, Bethie and Anna climbed up and up into the branches. A blizzard of gold maple leaves shook loose, and Anna watched them spin restlessly beneath her. Anna climbed up the last two branches.

"Here we are," she said.

"Yeah," Bethie said. Bethie's face was pale and tight. Anna wondered if she looked the same way.

Holding on to the maple tree, Anna peered

through the open window, into the shadows inside the room. There weren't any pale bodies in there. It was probably safe. Anna curved her fingers over the windowsill. Her knuckles became white from holding on so tightly. She reached inside the window with her foot. Anna closed her eyes and waited a minute to see if anything would happen inside, like the sound of moaning or feet clomping. But when the house remained silent, Anna swung her other foot in. Slowly, she groped for the floor. Anna felt the solid floor beneath her feet, waited for a few minutes, and then slid the rest of the way inside. She said, "Okay, Bethie. Come on in."

Anna kept her eyes closed. She heard the creak of the windowsill as Bethie slid inside. She heard the soft thud of Bethie's sneakers as Bethie landed on the floor. Anna felt the heat of Bethie's body and her warm breath on Anna's neck as Bethie stood very close behind her. Finally, Anna opened her eyes.

Bethie was the first to say it. "Wow!"

The room, a bedroom, was fully furnished. There was a large, intricately carved canopy bed. Above the bed was a rose silk canopy, now strung with cobwebs. There was a padded rocking chair beside the bed and a little nightstand with a lace doily. Two dressers stood on either side of the room, both with carved oak-leaf pulls. Best of all was a huge, full-length mirror. Anna walked quietly toward the mirror and stared at herself and the room behind her. Dust had softened the edges and colors of the room until the whole thing looked like the black-and-white background of an old picture. And there was Anna, reflected in the mirror, dressed in dirty sneakers and a red Mickey Mouse sweatshirt. In this old, dignified room, Anna looked out of place. Maybe it was a sign.

"Anna," Bethie whispered, "let's look in the dressers."

Anna walked toward her friend as Bethie pulled open a drawer. "There's nothing inside," she said. Anna opened another drawer, but it was empty too. They opened all the drawers in the first dresser and then the drawers in the other.

"They're all empty!" Anna said.

"The owners must have taken everything out," Bethie said, nodding her head positively.

"But if the owners took the things from inside

the drawers, then why didn't they take the furniture, too?"

Bethie paused for a minute, thinking. "Good question. Maybe somebody else took the things."

Anna said, "You mean someone who broke in, someone like us?"

"Yes. Maybe they weren't real thieves, just regular people. But I think it would be wrong to take things from this house. It would be stealing."

"Yes," Anna said. "We'll leave everything right where it is."

Bethie nodded solemnly. "But it is a good sign."

"What? That somebody took the things from the dresser?" Anna asked.

"Yes. If they took those things, then it means they got out of here safely. It proves that nothing bad will happen to us."

Relief pulsed through Anna, warm and welcome. Of course! It was proof the house was safe! But suddenly Anna's blood chilled. She gripped Bethie's hand. "Bethie," she said. "What if the thieves got out of the bedroom and got all the way downstairs *and then something happened to them*? What if they're downstairs now? What if they're dead?"

"They probably aren't there," Bethie said, and Anna wished she were convinced.

Bethie and Anna looked through the rest of the upstairs. There were two other bedrooms, both of them full of wonderful old furniture. But neither bedroom was cluttered with the little items that made a house homey. One bedroom was very small and furnished as a nursery. There was a cradle in it, a dresser, and a picture called "A Child's Prayer" with a chubby-legged girl kneeling down, praying. The other bedroom was larger, though not as large as the first bedroom, and the furniture was not as grand. It had a cherry bed with small balls on top of the posts. There were two dressers and a washstand. Maybe it was a guest room.

Now that Anna had seen the upstairs, she was convinced it was safe. But what was waiting downstairs? It was growing darker. The shadows on the wall were deepening and the girls were getting cold. Soon it would be too dark to see.

Determined, Anna clenched her fists tightly and said, "Come on, Bethie. Let's go downstairs." Anna dug her fingernails into the soft skin in the palm of her hand and began walking forward.

21

The stairs creaked beneath her weight. It must have been a long time since a person had walked down those stairs. Were they dangerous? Were they so old and soft she could fall through them? And, most frightening of all, what would Anna and Bethie find at the bottom? Whatever was there would have heard the creaking and would be waiting for them now.

There was a door at the bottom of the stairs. Anna didn't feel brave anymore, and she began to wonder why she had thought this was a good adventure in the first place. She huddled against Bethie. "You don't think there's really a ghost down here, do you?"

Bethie paused. "I don't think so." But Bethie's voice was trembly.

"Or dead bodies? You don't think the old owners were in the middle of moving when one of them died?"

"Or was killed," Bethie added.

"Which would explain why the furniture was left in the house."

"No. I'm practically sure that didn't happen." Slowly, Bethie reached toward the doorknob, turned it, and let the door swing open.

Anna and Bethie were amazed at what they found on the other side. There were no dead bodies—none that they could see, anyway. There were no ghosts. There was no one to get them. Instead, right in the middle of the dining room was a large, gaping hole. It was lucky they had been so careful when they opened the door. They could have fallen through.

"What made that hole?" Bethie asked, gripping Anna's hand so tightly that Anna couldn't feel the blood in it anymore.

"Maybe something exploded," Anna said.

"Maybe," Bethie said. "Or maybe the floor was just too old and heavy and it broke."

Anna nodded. "I think that was probably it. Do you think we could get past the hole and explore the rest of the house?"

"Maybe."

Anna considered that possibility for a minute. Now that she was downstairs she felt a lot braver. Bethie and Anna had explored over half of the house, and Anna was ready to come to the conclusion that the house was not haunted. And it would be fun to come back to the house later, to save the downstairs for another time. "Let's go home," she said.

"Okay," Bethie agreed. "We can explore the downstairs for our next Adventure Club."

As Bethie closed the door to go back up the stairs, Anna let her breath out in a rush. She hadn't been aware that she'd been holding it. Bethie and Anna began to climb the stairs. That's when they heard the sound. *Mmmmmmm. Mmmmmmm.* It was moaning.

Anna grabbed Bethie and Bethie grabbed Anna. "Did you hear that?" they both asked each other at once. Anna wanted to run. She wanted to bolt up the stairs, throw herself out of the window, and climb down the tree as fast as she could. But she felt as if her feet were stuck in cement. She could not lift them. She could not move.

The moaning continued. It was thin and high-pitched, almost like a baby's cry. It was the kind of sound that comes from a body that has no bones, Anna thought. *Mmmmmmmm. Mmmmmmmm.*

"Anna, I'm afraid," Bethie said. Her eyes were filling with tears.

Anna was not afraid to admit it. "Me too."

24

Clutching each other, moving as one person, they shuffled up another step together. Then they heard it again. *Mmmmmmmm Mmmmmmmm.*

"Anna!" Bethie screamed. "It isn't moaning! It's someone crying. Someone crying, 'Melea! Melea!' It's the ghost of Charles Streff calling Melea!"

Meeeea. Meeeea.

Anna paused to listen again. *Meeeeaw. Meeeeaw.*

Bethie screamed, "It's Charles calling Melea, Anna. What if he thinks we are Melea? What if he tries to get us?" Bethie began to run up the stairs.

But something about that cry didn't sound ghostly, and it didn't sound like "Melea, Melea," either. It sounded different, softer. It sounded alive. Anna listened again. *Meeeeeew.*

It was not a ghost! Anna was sure! And she thought she knew exactly what it was.

"Bethie!" Anna called, moving back down. Reluctantly, loyally, Bethie stopped at the top of the stairs. She turned to face her friend.

"Bethie, I don't think that sound is a ghost. It sounds like a kitten!"

Mmmreeeew.

But where was it? Eagerly, Anna opened the

25

door to the ground floor and looked around. There was no kitten there. Anna listened again.

Mmmreeew.

"Bethie," she said, "can you tell where the mewing is coming from?"

"It's coming from downstairs somewhere. I'm sure of that," Bethie said, returning down the stairs. Carefully, slowly, Anna and Bethie stepped around the hole and began to search in the dining room.

Mew, came the sound, more faintly.

"It's in here, Bethie. I know it!" cried Anna, following the sound.

Mraaiow!

"It's in the hole, Bethie!"

"It is!" Bethie agreed.

Immediately, Anna's heart swelled with love for the little kitten in the hole. How frightened it must be! How hungry! Anna always had a special place in her heart for little animals in trouble. She had certainly been in trouble often enough herself. She knew how it felt. This kitten needed her! Anna wanted to rescue it—she had to! But how? How could she get the kitten up without falling in herself?

An idea was beginning to form in Anna's mind. "Bethie," she began, "I know how to rescue a person on thin ice, and this broken floor seems like thin ice, doesn't it?"

"Yes," agreed Bethie.

"Here's what we can do. We'll stretch ourselves along the floor. You hold on to my hand, and I'll slide across the floor till I get to the hole. Then I'll reach inside and pull out the kitten."

"Okay, Anna," Bethie said.

Anna thought, There is no friend truer than Bethie. My plan is dangerous, yet Bethie is willing to go along with it. I may have many friends in my life, but none will be more loyal than Bethie. Anna smiled to show Bethie how much she appreciated her friendship.

"Okay," Bethie said, "let's get down slowly." The friends knelt on the floor and then spread themselves against it, holding hands. The floor was cold, and it was gritty with dirt. Anna held her head up a little so her cheek would not touch the floor. Then she slid slowly, slowly toward the hole.

It was pretty dark now, and it was difficult to see inside the hole. Anna looked carefully, scanning the dark corners and fallen debris. There

it was! Anna could just make out a small, gray kitten in the dim light. "I see it!" Anna cried to Bethie.

"Oh, Anna," Bethie cried. "Is it really there?"

"It is!" Anna said.

"Can you reach it?"

"No. It's too far down." The kitten was way, way below, far too low for Anna to reach. What would she do?

As Anna and Bethie lay on the old, sagging floor, they heard a sound that made their hearts leap to their throats.

Creeeeeak. Snap!

Anna and Bethie clung to each other desperately. But there was no way they could stop the terrible groaning and crashing. Anna thought, If I die, I'll go to heaven because I was doing a good deed. And that was the last thing she remembered.

Anna felt almost like she was dreaming, but not quite. She thought, This is what it feels like to be dead. I am dead. Heaven is nice, but not as nice as I'd hoped. It's bright and misty, like when you're up in an airplane. But there aren't very many people here. Anna was encouraged when she felt an angel grab her arm and shake it.

"Why are you shaking me?" she asked the angel, happy that there was someone else in heaven with her.

The angel spoke in Bethie's voice. "Wake up, Anna!" Bethie was in heaven too! The angel, Bethie, spoke again. "Come on, Anna, open your eyes."

Anna was surprised to find that her eyes weren't already open. She thought they were. When Anna pulled her lids up, she saw Bethie, her face dark and dusty, her eyes frightened.

"Are you okay?" Bethie asked.

"Yes. But I thought I was in heaven. Where are we?"

Bethie took a quick, deep breath. "We're in the hole. Don't you remember?" Then Bethie screamed, "Anna, do you have amnesia? Please don't have amnesia!"

Anna said, "No, I don't have amnesia." When Anna looked around, when she saw the deep, dark hole they were in, she wished she did. Anna shifted her weight and discovered that there were many parts of her that hurt a lot. Anna flexed her feet and her hands and she wiggled her shoulders. She didn't think anything was broken. Luckily, Anna and Bethie had fallen onto an old carpet. Otherwise . . . well, Anna didn't want to think about it.

"Bethie, where's the kitten?" she asked suddenly.

"Over here," Bethie said. The little gray kitten was curled up against the back of Anna's legs.

"Oh, you poor little thing," Anna said, reaching toward the kitten, picking it up and stroking it gently with her cheek, plunging her nose into its downy fur. How light the kitten was. Why, it didn't weigh more than a teacup! It was thin and very bony, but it was purring. Anna felt a new determination. There were many times she had dreamed of saving an animal, and now she had done it . . . almost. She couldn't very well get to the kitten and then not bring it to safety. No, she had to find a way to get out of this place! Anna squinted at Bethie. It was very dark, and she couldn't see her very well. "How do you think we can get out of here?" Anna asked Bethie.

"I don't know," Bethie said miserably. "The opening is too far up. Even if I stand on your shoulders, I'm sure I couldn't reach it."

"Let's try," suggested Anna. Anna planted her legs firmly against the highest mound of rubble in the hole, and Bethie climbed up onto Anna's shoulders. "Can you reach?" Anna asked.

"No," Bethie said in a small, quiet voice. Then she climbed down.

It was very dark in that hole, and it was damp and cold. Anna picked up the little gray kitten and put it inside her sweatshirt to keep it warm. In return, Anna felt some comfort from the purring, warm little bulge.

"Maybe in the morning we can see well enough to pile some boards up to reach the top," Anna suggested.

"Maybe," Bethie said.

Neither friend spoke her worst fears aloud: What if they didn't make it to morning? What if they died in the night, frozen, alone in that dark, horrible place?

Anna's thoughts became warm and misty as she thought about her family at home, snuggled in the little gray house with the widow's walk. How she wished she were with them now! How she wished she were sitting down to dinner with her family, eating pot roast, talking about her day. Anna's stomach rumbled as she thought about the pot roast, warm from the oven. She was so cold and hungry! Anna closed her eyes and imagined the conversation at the kitchen table.

"Isn't this the day you get your Progress Reports from school, girls?" Daddy would ask.

"Yes," Anna would say. "Here's mine."

Daddy would open the envelope very slowly. Anna knew what the report said, because she had looked as soon as she was out of the school doors. After all, Miss Crystal must have wanted her to look. If she hadn't, she would have sealed the envelope.

Daddy would read out loud.

Dear Mr. and Mrs. Skoggen,

Anna is a bright and creative member of our classroom. She contributes eagerly to class discussions. When Anna reads aloud, she does so dramatically and energetically. All of us love to hear Anna read.

Anna socializes well with her classmates. We

33

*are working on teaching her to socialize at appro-
priate times.*

Sheila Crystal

"Our Anna is certainly a gifted student," Mom would say, smiling at her younger daughter.

"Yes, to think she's such a good reader! She must take after you, Helen. You've always had a way with reading aloud," Daddy would say.

Mom would smile with pride. "Our Anna! A dramatic reader. A student beloved by her classmates."

"But what about me?" Kimberly would say. "What about *my* Progress Report?"

"I'm sure yours is very nice too," Daddy would say.

Anna felt she had the best family in the world. Anna thought of Daddy, bony and tall. She thought of wrapping her arms around his neck, and she thought of him patting her gently. And Mom! She was so kind and beautiful. Anna knew that all the people who came to Mom's bookmobile thought she was wonderful too. Even Kimberly was nice. Now Anna wished she had been nicer to her sister and had not told Kimberly her nail polish looked like rotten fruit.

What would Anna's family do without Anna's cheerful face? And her classmates! Everyone enjoyed hearing Anna read aloud. What would they look forward to every day if they couldn't hear her read?

Feeling very miserable, Anna and Bethie began to cry. Huge tears ran down their dirty cheeks.

"Help!" Bethie began to shout.

"Help! Help!" Anna yelled too.

But no one knew where Bethie and Anna were. This was an old, deserted house. Who would hear them? Who would walk so deep into the country, especially at night? Who would come to the rescue of the two best friends and their kitten?

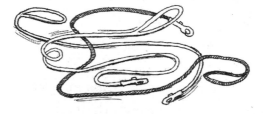

3

THE RESCUE

"Yoo-hoo!"

"Did you hear that?" asked Anna.

"No," Bethie said, between cries. "What did you hear?"

"Somebody said, 'Yoo-hoo.'"

Maybe someone was outside! Maybe someone could hear them. They cried, loudly, "HELP! HEEEEELP!"

Soon they heard someone pound against the door of the house. "Yoo-hoo!" the someone called again. "Is anybody there?"

"WE ARE!" yelled Anna as loudly as she could. "We fell in a hole and we can't get out!"

"Well, hold on, then," the somebody called. "I'll have to break these old boards away."

Anna and Bethie heard scraping and pounding and the bashing of a rock against wood. After a while they heard the welcome sound of feet walking on bare wooden floors. At last they weren't alone.

"Oh my, oh my, oh my!" the someone said. "We're in some kind of pickle, aren't we?" The person's voice was brisk and chuckly . . . and somehow familiar. It sounded like . . . could it be Anna's Cat Lady?

"Mrs. Sarafiny, is that you?"

"Why, yes indeed. And who is that?"

Anna jumped up and down. "It's Anna, the red-headed girl, and my friend Bethie."

"Anna!" came Mrs. Sarafiny's voice, warm and welcoming. Anna felt a deep affection for wonderful, squishy Mrs. Sarafiny, her rescuer. "I'll have you out of there in a jiffy."

Mraaiow.

"There's no use carrying on, darlings. We have to untangle ourselves so we can help Anna and

Bethie," said the voice.

Mew. Mew. Mrmrmrmr.

"That's right, Nancy. Now listen to your sister, darlings. She's telling you to cooperate. Yes. Cooperation is what we must have."

There was more mewing and some huffing and puffing. Pretty soon Mrs. Sarafiny said, "I'm taking the leashes off my children here. Then I'll snap the leashes together and lower the whole thing down to you, like a long chain." Soon a snapped-together chain of leashes fell into the hole. Mrs. Sarafiny said, "I just knew something like this was going to happen. Nancy told me to watch out for the Martians. And now look what they've done!"

Martians? What was Mrs. Sarafiny talking about? "We have the leashes," Anna called up, "but what do we do with them?"

"I'm going to fasten them to this door handle here," said Mrs. Sarafiny, "and then you can step in each loop and pull yourselves up. I think it'll do the trick. Here, I'll shine the flashlight on the leashes for you."

"Who's going to go first?" Bethie asked.

Anna didn't know whether the leashes would

hold together. She didn't know if a climbing person would be too heavy. Then the leashes would break and the person would fall. But Anna felt responsible—the whole thing had been her idea, after all. So Anna said, "I will."

"Okay," Bethie said.

Anna thought about how she would tell the story of tonight's adventure, once she was out of this hole. She imagined the part where she'd say, "A long chain of leashes was tied together. Someone had to climb the chain. Whoever it was had to be very brave, because no one knew if the chain would break. I volunteered."

Gently, delicately, the kitten wriggled against Anna's skin. The kitten's movement felt good, like the tug on a fishing line that shows there's something live under the water. "We're going to climb now," Anna said to the kitten. She tucked her sweatshirt into her pants so the kitten wouldn't fall out. Mrs. Sarafiny was saving Anna, and Anna was saving the kitten. After this, there would be a special bond uniting all of them. Anna would always be grateful to Mrs. Sarafiny. The kitten would always be grateful to Anna.

Anna began to climb the ladder of leashes.

Afraid to look back, afraid to look forward, Anna continued to lift herself up. Her hands and arms trembled, partly from exhaustion and partly from fear. What if the leashes broke and Anna fell again? What if the floor crumbled when Anna got to the top? Anna's head rose over the top of the hole. Soon she would be safe! At last, Anna cleared the hole and carefully slid on her side onto the floor with one hand on the kitten in her sweatshirt. She was completely exhausted.

Anna looked around. She could just make out a large, bulky shadow—Mrs. Sarafiny—and a bunch of little shadows—the cats! Mrs. Sarafiny and her cats floated toward Anna. Soon Anna felt plump arms lift her up, and she smelled baby-powdery skin. "Are you all right, sweetie?" Mrs. Sarafiny asked.

"Yes," Anna said, but she couldn't stop trembling. Mrs. Sarafiny held her close, and her cats rubbed against Anna's legs.

"Bethie," Anna called. "It's not as scary as it looks. I'm fine, and you will be too."

"Are you sure?" Bethie said. Her voice sounded far away.

"Yes."

Anna heard the soft creak of leather pulling against itself. It seemed to take a long, long time before Bethie's head came up over the rim of the hole.

"Bethie!" Anna called when Bethie was safely at the top. And then Anna began to cry. Mrs. Sarafiny bent over and held the two friends, one in each sturdy arm. "There, there, darlings. Everything's all right now." Mrs. Sarafiny patted Anna and Bethie gently on their heads.

After a while their cries slowed to sharp, noisy gulps and then they stopped. It felt so good, so deliciously good, to be safe. The little gray kitten popped its head out from the top of Anna's sweatshirt. It cried, long and trembly, *Mmreeeeew!*

"Hello," said Mrs. Sarafiny, shining the flashlight on the tiny, gray head. "What have we here?" The kitten crawled out of Anna's shirt, and Mrs. Sarafiny cradled it gently in her plump hand. "My goodness!—she's so thin!"

She. The kitten was a girl. "What's your kitten's name?" Mrs. Sarafiny asked.

"Her name?" Anna had just read about Princess Caroline of Monaco in her school newspaper. A royal name seemed just right for this special kitten. "I'm going to call her Caroline," said Anna. "But I haven't told her her name yet. I just found her."

"Oh my! Where did you find Caroline?"

Anna and Bethie explained the whole story. Anna was tempted to exaggerate, to make the story more interesting. But for once she found that the truth was dramatic enough. It didn't need any additions at all. When she finished, Mrs. Sarafiny said, "My my my my my. What a commotion!" She shook her head, and her fuzzy hair shimmered in the light of the flashlight. "Of course, I knew something like this would happen, what with the Martians and all."

Bethie leaned over to Anna. "What does Mrs. Sarafiny mean, *the Martians?*" she whispered.

"I don't know," Anna whispered back. Anna knew it was rude to whisper in front of someone, but she really wondered about the Martian thing herself.

Mrs. Sarafiny leaned over confidentially. "You know, girls, it was no accident that I came here. Nancy told me to come. She has a sixth sense, you see. She can tell when things are going to happen. She knew there would be trouble with the Martians tonight, and she knew just where to find it."

"I see," said Anna, not seeing at all but not wanting to say it.

"You'll be happy to know I've come prepared." Mrs. Sarafiny reached into her straw Manzanillo bag and pulled out a little pile of candy bars. "Help yourselves, girls," she said.

Bethie chose a toffee candy bar. Anna took one with peanuts, chocolate, and caramel. She bit into it and tasted the sweet chocolate on her tongue. "Mmmmm," she said. Anna crunched the nuts. This was the nuttiest, chocolatiest candy bar Anna had ever eaten. She would never forget how wonderful it tasted.

"I'll bet little Caroline is hungry too," Mrs. Sarafiny said, and reached into her bag again. "Voilà! Liver." With quick fingers, Mrs. Sarafiny opened a small foil-wrapped package. "When one travels with cats, one never forgets liver."

Hungrily, greedily, Caroline chewed into the liver. She made little clucking sounds of pleasure with each bite. Mrs. Sarafiny had to pluck the other cats out of Caroline's way. They wanted the liver too.

Mrs. Sarafiny reached into her bag again and brought out another foil-wrapped bundle. "Take this home and give it to Caroline later tonight."

Mrs. Sarafiny leaned forward and grunted a bit as she pulled herself up. "I just can't move the way I used to, girls," she said. "Getting old is the pits."

Anna smiled. Mrs. Sarafiny didn't talk the way grown-ups usually talked. Anna had to admit the Martian thing was strange, but she really liked Mrs. Sarafiny.

Mrs. Sarafiny gathered her six cats and snapped their leashes back on. "All right, my darlings," she said. "It's time to go home."

Home! Anna couldn't wait to get there. Anna tucked Caroline back into her sweatshirt. She wrapped her arms across her chest, partly to support the little kitten and partly to keep both of them warm.

"Come on, troops," said Mrs. Sarafiny, charging ahead, shining the flashlight along the way. Mrs. Sarafiny's cats walked in six different directions, tails up. They wove in and out, tangling the leashes, and Mrs. Sarafiny stumbled. Patiently, she bent down, untangled the leashes, and walked ahead, through the front door to the overgrown yard outside.

"Can you girls make it home okay?" she asked.

"Sure," Bethie said. "We're fine now." At that, Caroline popped her head out of Anna's sweatshirt. She meowed loudly.

Mrs. Sarafiny laughed joyfully. "So you are. Well then, toodles," she called, and proceeded to lead her little cat parade away.

Anna held up Caroline's soft little paw and waved it at Mrs. Sarafiny. "'Bye," she said.

"And thanks," Bethie called. Then Bethie spoke softly to Anna. "Are you taking her home with you?"

"Yes," Anna said.

"I thought Kimberly was allergic."

Anna didn't know what to say to that. She had begun to worry about taking Caroline home herself. Mom and Daddy had said, "Absolutely no cats." But Anna had saved Caroline! Surely Mom and Daddy wouldn't mean "no" to Caroline. Anna had to admit Kimberly's allergies might be a problem. But Caroline was such a small kitten, with such a little bit of cat dander. Besides, Anna doubted whether Kimberly was really allergic

46

anyway. Maybe it was her imagination. Maybe the *thought* of cats made Kimberly sick. Suddenly Anna had a plan. Anna would hide Caroline. If Kimberly didn't know Caroline was there, she wouldn't be sick. Then Anna could prove that Kimberly's allergies were all in her imagination, and Anna could keep Caroline forever.

Anna thought about how she might sneak Caroline into the house. She would have to hide her in the garage first, until the family was asleep. Then she could move Caroline inside.

It took a long time for Anna and Bethie to make their way to Anna's house. Then Anna turned and said, "Good-bye, Bethie. I'll see you tomorrow."

Bethie grinned at Anna under the lamplight. "Yeah. Anna, this was the best adventure we ever had!"

Anna smiled back. Her heart filled with love for her very best friend. Only a friend as true as Bethie would view tonight's events as an adventure.

Anna and Bethie gave each other the Best Friends Handshake and said good-bye. Then Anna opened the garage door very quietly and sneaked inside with Caroline. It was cold in the garage, so Caroline would need something to wrap around her. Anna searched for something soft and warm. There, on the backseat of the car! Kimberly's Big Rock Cafe sweatshirt was perfect! Anna opened the car door and arranged Caroline on the front passenger seat, wrapped in Kimberly's sweatshirt. Then she put a little more of the liver on the seat.

Mr-r-r-r-r.

"It's okay, Princess Caroline," she said. "I'll be back soon. You just stay here." Carefully, Anna closed the car door and walked to the house. She paused on the front porch and thought about the joyful homecoming she would receive. She thought about her family gathered around her, happy she was safe, eager to hear every word of her adventure. Anna opened the door.

"Anna!" cried Mom, rushing toward her, Daddy and Kimberly not far behind. Mom opened her arms and swept Anna into them. Mom hugged Anna tightly. "Oh, Anna," she said, kissing Anna's cheek again and again. "You're all right. But Anna, what happened? Where were you?"

And Anna began to tell. She found again that

the truth was quite dramatic and she didn't need to exaggerate. So, except for the part about Caroline, Anna told the story exactly as it had happened.

When Anna got to the part about Mrs. Sarafiny, Daddy said, "The Cat Lady?"

"Yes. Mrs. Sarafiny has six cats."

Kimberly butted in. "The Cat Lady is a little bit weird. I mean, really! Anybody who has six cats on a leash is on the edge. Plus she wears *very* unusual clothes—things that are out of season. And hats made of bread wrappers! She's just not normal."

Anna was getting sick of hearing about normal.

"In my experience," Anna said firmly, "Mrs. Sarafiny is quite normal. If *I* could have six cats, I would." Anna looked pointedly at her "allergic" sister.

Kimberly sniffed and said, "I rest my case." Then Kimberly added, "I wonder what Mrs. Sarafiny was doing way out there in the first place?"

"Just walking her cats," Anna said. Anna sensed that it was best not to explain that Mrs. Sarafiny's cat had led her to the old house because of the Martians. The Martian thing made Mrs. Sarafiny sound too weird. If Anna told the whole truth about why Mrs. Sarafiny was there, then her family would worry. Anna had always believed that not telling everything wasn't really lying. It was saving someone from needless worry.

"Whether Mrs. Sarafiny is 'normal' or not doesn't really matter," Mom said. "She rescued you, and we're all grateful. I'll call her tomorrow and thank her myself." Mom's eyes filled with tears. "We're all so glad you're safe, Anna!"

"Yes, Anna, you sure gave us a fright. I didn't know what to think when I read your note, especially the part about 'No matter what, remember that I love you.' And then, when you didn't come home . . ." Daddy shook his head grimly.

Kimberly said, "I'm glad you're home too." Kimberly really did look glad. Maybe it wasn't so bad, Anna thought, to shake up your family now and then. It reminded them how much they liked you.

The Skoggen family walked into the kitchen, Daddy's long arm wrapped around Anna's shoulder. She really did have the best family in the world.

50

"I'll bet you're starving, Anna," Mom said, bustling around in the kitchen, putting waxed paper over Anna's plate of pot roast to warm in the microwave. Anna liked being the center of attention. She liked having everyone hug her and fuss over her. It was obvious they really cared about her. Maybe they would not scold her for breaking into a deserted house. But when Daddy's face grew serious and he folded his hands in front of him, Anna knew a scolding was in store.

"Anna," Daddy began, "what you did was very dangerous. You could have been badly hurt, even killed." There was nothing Daddy enjoyed more than giving a long speech, like the editorials he wrote for the *Door County Advocate*. But Anna had already heard an editorial from Kimberly today, and that was enough. So Anna thought about Princess Caroline instead.

Daddy cleared his throat, something he always did at the end of his speech. "Ahem. In conclusion, Anna, always remember that you alone are responsible for your safety. In the future, do not be so foolish. And I would prefer it if you didn't speak with Mrs. Sarafiny anymore."

Anna suddenly felt a lump in her throat. She

51

kept her eyes on the floor. "I won't, Daddy," she said softly.

Later that night, Anna waited for the familiar sound of Kimberly's snoring. Then she wrapped herself in her robe, stepped into her slippers, and silently walked down to the garage to rescue Caroline from the car.

There was Caroline, wrapped sweetly in Kimberly's sweatshirt, her little mouth curved upward in a pleasant kitten smile. The packet of liver, partially eaten, lay open on the seat. Anna picked up Caroline delicately and carried her up to her room. She threw Kimberly's sweatshirt onto the floor of the closet. Anna lay down on her bed and put Caroline beside her cheek, stroking her sleek little head, running her finger down her nose. *Rrrrrrr*. Caroline was purring so loudly that Anna was afraid she would wake Kimberly, so she tucked Caroline beneath the covers. Caroline crept to the back of Anna's knees and curled up there.

Despite the comforting warmth of Caroline beside her, Anna's stomach felt cold and twisty. Falling into the hole had been scary. Then Anna became aware of voices coming from downstairs.

"You really are too permissive with Anna, Helen," Daddy said loudly.

"*I'm* permissive. You mean the children are *my* responsibility? What happened to mutual parenting, Paul?" Mom's voice was shrill and high.

"You know what I meant, Helen. *We* are too permissive."

"I think you said exactly what you meant, Paul. You think when things go wrong with the children that it's my responsibility to stop them."

"No. It's just that you must realize the seriousness of this situation. Anna could have gotten badly hurt—even killed."

"I see," said Mom. It sounded like icicles were hanging on her words. "Then it *is* my responsibility to see that Anna doesn't get in trouble."

"I didn't say that." Daddy's words were icy too.

Now Mom was shouting. "That's exactly what you said, Paul. You want me to take the blame for every crazy thing Anna does."

Mom thought Anna's actions were crazy! Did that mean Mom didn't love Anna?

"Well I won't!" Mom continued, still shouting. "Anna has a mind of her own—she always has. It's not easy to keep an eye on her, because I never know what she's going to do next. Paul, Anna is our daughter, OURS! Not just mine."

Did that mean Mom was sorry Anna was her daughter? Anna's stomach felt hot and bubbly. Her skin hurt.

Mom shouted, "Say something, Paul! Don't just sit there, like a bump. Show some emotion. Show some concern. Show *something*! I can't stand it when you're like this."

Anna covered her ears with her pillow. She hated it when Mom and Daddy argued. It made her feel afraid. Anna had begun to notice that Mom and Daddy argued a lot lately. Was something terribly wrong? Falling into the hole proved that bad things do happen. Suddenly Anna felt as if all the air had been squeezed out of her lungs. Were Mom and Daddy going to get a divorce?

Please, please don't let that happen, Anna begged silently. Anna reached beneath the covers to pet Caroline, but she found that even that did not help.

4

TAKING
CAROLINE ALONG

Anna woke up early, before anyone else, her head still fuzzy from sleep. She felt Caroline, warm against her legs. Anna thought, Caroline would love me if I were sick or crabby or naughty. Caroline would love me even if I got into very serious trouble. Then the pleasant thoughts about Caroline stopped with a thud. Anna remembered Mom and Daddy's argument. They had argued because of Anna. Anna didn't want to think about it, but her stomach felt cold and twisty anyway. More than ever, Anna was determined to stay out of trouble. She would be very good in school. She would not make big messes or be late or argue with Kimberly. Most of all, Anna would be a responsible pet owner. Maybe, if Anna was really careful, Mom and Daddy wouldn't argue again.

Anna would have preferred to stay in bed, snuggled deep beneath the covers. But she had to get Caroline settled before the rest of her family got up. So Anna reached beneath the covers and pulled out the sleepy kitten. Caroline stretched, pushing her legs in front of her, narrowing her eyes to slits. Caroline was thin and bony, Anna had to admit, so it would be important to keep her well fed. Her fur was soft and downy, like the hair on a baby's head. Caroline's eyes were a brilliant green, the color of the lush green moss that grew between the bricks along Anna's walk. But Anna liked Caroline's feet best of all. The two front feet were white, like booties, and the tiny little claws were slivers.

Anna tucked Caroline into her pajama top while she prepared a hiding place. Anna had thought about where she could keep Caroline while she was at school. The best spot, she decided, was the hidey-hole. At the back of the closet, behind all the clothes, was a false wall. It was fastened shut with knobs that could turn to slide the wall open. Behind the wall was a low attic, a hidey-hole where Mom and Daddy stored suitcases, old boxes of clothes, a cedar chest full of sweaters, and Anna's old toys. Sometimes Anna and Bethie had secret meetings in the hidey-hole. There was a light in there, a bare bulb with a pull string, but they always used flashlights. Hardly anyone but Bethie and Anna used the hidey-hole, except for storage, so Anna felt it was the perfect spot to hide Caroline.

Anna slipped her jacket over her pajamas and went outside. It was cold out, so she walked to the sandbox quickly. Anna found an old pan by the sandbox and scooped some sand into it. That would work for kitty litter, at least until Anna could get the real thing. Anna brought the sand pan back inside. She set it on the kitchen floor and let Caroline dig until she figured out what it was for. Then Anna put leftover chicken in a dish and poured some milk on top of it. This would be Caroline's breakfast, though personally Anna thought chicken and milk was disgusting. Then

Anna carried the sand pan, the breakfast dish, and Caroline to the hidey-hole. She pulled Caroline out from her pajama top and set her next to the breakfast dish.

Mrraaaiow.

"You're welcome," Anna said. Caroline attacked the chicken as if it were alive, pouncing on it and then gulping it down. When her paws got in the milk, Caroline shook them and sprayed milk all over. Anna would have to clean up the mess later. When she was finished, Caroline licked herself all over. Anna lifted Caroline up and kissed her gently on the nose. Then she slipped out of the hidey-hole to get dressed.

"Where were you, Anna?" asked Kimberly, stretching in bed.

"I was just in the closet, getting something," Anna explained.

Kimberly sat up. Her eyes were red and puffy and her skin was splotchy red, probably because she was still tired. "Uhh," Kimberly groaned, falling backward to the pillow again.

Mom poked her head through the doorway. "I let everybody sleep a little later this morning because of all the excitement last night. But now

58

you'll have to hustle. I'll be taking you to school today." Then Mom ran downstairs.

Kimberly pulled the covers over her head. She said, from inside, "I can't believe it's morning. Uhhhh," she groaned again.

"Come on, Kimberly," said Anna, reaching under the covers to pull Kimberly out.

"I'm up!" cried Kimberly, slowly rolling out of bed. Kimberly looked in the mirror. She stared at her swollen eyes and blotchy skin. Her mouth flew open in disbelief. "What happened to me? I can't go to school looking like this."

Anna felt she should defend her sister. "You look fine to me, Kimberly. In fact, you look beautiful!"

"No I don't. I look like a dork." Kimberly sat down suddenly. "Maybe I'm getting my period. Maybe this is what your face looks like when you have a period." Kimberly groaned, "Ohhhh. Am I going to look like this every month? I'll have to be a nun or an old maid because no one will ever date me looking like this."

Sometimes Kimberly really exaggerated. "You look fine, Kimberly, really you do. Your face just looks sleepy. It'll look better after breakfast."

Anna knew that was the kind of reassuring thing a mother or very wise sister would say, and she was proud of herself for thinking of it.

"I hope you're right," said Kimberly. Then Kimberly began rummaging around in her drawer, looking for something.

Anna said, "Can I help you, Kimberly?" That was another thing a wise sister would say. Anna was proud that she had become so thoughtful and reassuring. When you are a pet owner, you become more mature.

"I'm looking for my Big Rock Cafe sweatshirt. I want to wear it today. Oh! I think I left it in the car last night."

Anna picked up the sweatshirt she had thrown on the floor of the closet the night before and spun it around, waving it like a banner. "Here it is! I brought it inside for you!" By now Kimberly must be noticing how responsible Anna had become. Soon Kimberly would discuss it with Mom and Daddy. They would talk about how mature Anna was and they would wonder why. Then, when Anna proved that Kimberly was not allergic, they would realize that Anna had changed because she was a pet owner.

Especially now, when Mom and Daddy were arguing so much, it was important for Anna to act as mature as possible. When Anna thought about Mom and Daddy fighting, last night's cold, shivery feeling crept inside her again. She must act grown-up and stay out of trouble. She must never worry Mom and Daddy, or give them reason to argue with each other. Then maybe they would get along again and be a happy family.

During breakfast, Kimberly began to sneeze. When she said thickly, "Pass the cereal, Adda," Mom felt Kimberly's head for fever.

"What's wrong, dear?" she asked. "Are you coming down with a cold?"

"I guess so," said Kimberly. "I didd't sleep very well last dight. I kept dreabig about babies cryig."

Had Kimberly heard Caroline mewing? Anna's heart sank. Could her cold be . . . allergies?

"Well, Kimberly, you don't look very well," said Mom. Kimberly's face was still blotchy and her eyes were swollen. "But I hate to see you stay home unless you have a fever. If you feel worse at school, call Daddy. He'll take you home."

Anna thought about Caroline. She missed

61

having her inside her shirt. It would be a long day at school, and Caroline would really miss Anna. Maybe she would think Anna would never come back. Kittens are too young to understand about people leaving for a little while and then returning. Now that Anna was responsible and mature, she felt she should come up with a solution to this problem.

Of course! Anna could tuck Caroline into her shirt and take her to school. Anna could keep Caroline warm and she could keep her from becoming lonely. Anna was aware that animals were not allowed in school, but Caroline was so small, no one would see her. Anna was positive that this was the wise thing to do. So, after breakfast, Anna hurried to the hidey-hole to get Caroline.

Mrreeew.

"Princess Caroline," she explained, "I'm taking you to school. You aren't allowed there, so you must be very quiet and sit very still." Anna tucked Caroline inside her sweatshirt and hurried downstairs.

In the garage, Anna hesitated before she got into the car. Anna usually preferred to sit in front. She was closer to Mom there, and she could see the traffic better. The person who rode in back was usually the last person to see something. But today Anna didn't want Kimberly or Mom to get a good look at her, so she slid into the back where she would be alone. She mustn't call attention to herself, not in the car and not at school. She would not volunteer answers today and she would not offer to read aloud, even if her classmates looked forward to it.

Anna heard the kitchen door slam as Mom and Kimberly entered the garage. Mom got in first and put her key into the ignition. Kimberly opened the front door, her arms piled high with books. She paused for a moment, and suddenly Anna remembered the little foil packet, full of leftover pieces of liver. Anna had meant to take it back inside last night.

Thud! Kimberly sat down heavily on the seat and on the liver. "What's this?" she asked, moving slightly off her seat. She pulled off pieces of the liver, now mashed into her skirt. "Yuck!" she cried. "Gross! What *is* this?" Kimberly held the liver in her fingers for a moment. Then she tried to shake it off.

"I have no idea what that is, Kimberly," Mom said. Then she sniffed the air. "Why, it smells like liver, of all things." Mom shook her head. "But that's silly. What would liver be doing in our car?" Mom started the car. "Well, it must be mud or something, Kimberly. Just wipe it off with a tissue."

Kimberly began to cry. "I look disgustig! My dose is ruddy add my eyes are swolled and my skid looks like it's full of zits. Add dow I have sobethig horrible stuck to by skirt!"

Anna knew it was her fault. She felt terrible. But she also knew that forgetting the liver on the seat was the last irresponsible thing she would ever do.

They picked up Bethie on the way. Bethie slid into the backseat beside Anna.

"Hi, Bethie," Kimberly said thickly.

"Hello, Kimberly. Do you have a cold?"

"I guess," Kimberly said.

Bethie whispered to Anna, "Did you tell your family about Caroline yet?"

Anna cupped her hand to Bethie's ear. She whispered as softly as possible, so no one else would hear. "No."

Bethie whispered back. "Is Kimberly allergic?"

Anna whispered, "No. Well, maybe. I don't know."

Bethie's eyes mirrored Anna's sad and fearful ones. But she said, "Well, she's probably not. I'm sure she'll be fine."

Just then, Anna and Bethie saw Mrs. Sarafiny. She was walking her cats, and she was carrying an umbrella. The umbrella was open and held above her head, which was strange, because it wasn't raining. Anna and Bethie waved enthusiastically at their rescuer, but Mrs. Sarafiny didn't see them.

Anna looked at Kimberly and Mom in the front seat. They were chattering away and looked too busy to pay attention to the best friends in the backseat. Anna patted the bump in her shirt and whispered to Bethie, "I'm bringing Caroline to school."

"But it isn't show and tell," Bethie said.

"I know. That's why I'm not going to show and I'm not going to tell. I'm going to keep Caroline a secret."

Bethie looked unconvinced.

"Caroline's a very good little kitten," Anna

assured her. "She'll hold perfectly still. I'll keep her in my shirt during school, and we can let her play in the grass during recess. Besides, she's so young and she had such a bad experience in that hole. I think it would be very harmful to leave her alone right now."

Bethie still didn't look convinced, but Anna was sure Caroline would be fine.

At school, Mom slid the car to a stop. "Here you are, girls," she said. Anna, Bethie, and Kimberly got out. Anna moved quickly, her arms folded over her kitten, and Kimberly plodded slowly. Mom looked worriedly at Kimberly. "Don't hesitate to call Daddy if you feel worse, Kimberly," she called out.

Anna didn't want Kimberly to worry Mom, either, so she threw her arm over Kimberly's shoulder. "Kimberly will be fine, Mom. I'll watch out for her. I'll make sure she's okay."

Mom looked up, surprised. "Anna, you sound so mature," she said.

Anna smiled, pleased that Mom had noticed. "I'll take care of everything," she said in a reassuring tone. "Don't worry about a thing." Anna noticed that Mom did not look especially reassured,

66

but in time she knew Mom would learn to trust her.

"Thanks for the ride, Mrs. Skoggen," Bethie said as Mom drove away.

In the classroom, everyone swarmed toward Bethie and Anna. Collin said, "Anna, tell us about the old house. Do you really think it was haunted?"

Kirsten said, "Maybe a ghost pushed you down the hole. Tell us about the hole, Bethie."

Anna asked, "How did you find out about the haunted house?"

Claire said, "Kimberly called my sister, and she told me. I told everybody else."

Anna heard the *tap tap tap* of Miss Crystal's heels as she walked down the hall. When Miss Crystal entered the room, Claire told her about the haunted house.

"My! What an experience!" Then Miss Crystal told the class, "You know, we're doing a unit on public speaking. I think it would be a wonderful opportunity to hear Bethie and Anna tell us what happened in that deserted house. Would you like to do that later, girls?"

How Anna longed to tell her classmates about

67

the haunted house, especially the part about saving a kitten. Miss Crystal loved animals too. She would be very proud that Anna had been so brave. But Anna didn't dare speak. What if someone noticed Caroline while Anna was talking? So Anna said very quietly, "I think Bethie should tell the story."

Miss Crystal looked surprised. "Are you sure, Anna?" she asked.

Anna just couldn't stand in front of the class with Caroline in her shirt! So she said, "I'm sure, Miss Crystal. Let Bethie tell the story."

Anna looked down at the small bulge in her sweatshirt. It was a big responsibility to have a pet. Sometimes you had to give up things you really wanted to do. Anna sighed. But probably it was worth it.

Caroline was very still during roll call and lunch count. She was not so still during the math quiz. She kept plucking at Anna's skin with her sharp little claws. "Ouch!" Anna said once, but she covered her mouth with her hand before any sound came out. It was very difficult to concentrate on numbers, and Anna was worried she wouldn't get a very good grade on this quiz.

When the test was over, Anna was sorry she'd taken Caroline to school.

After math, Miss Crystal made the introduction. "Boys and girls, Miss Bethie Anderson is going to tell us a true story." Miss Crystal swept her arm open grandly. "And now, introducing Miss Bethie Anderson."

The class clapped enthusiastically. Bethie walked to the front of the class and began to tell the story. "Well," she said, "there was this meeting of the Adventure Club. Anna and I are in the Adventure Club. Anyway, we decided to explore a real haunted house."

We didn't decide, thought Anna. *I* decided. It was my idea. Caroline began to squirm under Anna's sweatshirt.

"So we climbed this tree and got in through the second-story window." Bethie was telling the story all wrong. She should speak more dramatically and use her hands more. She's telling the story too fast. She should draw it out, for emphasis. Anna felt hot. It was a sunny morning and the room was full of light. Caroline was beginning to feel too warm against Anna's skin.

Meeeeew. Meeeeew.

69

Anna's hand shot to her stomach to cover the noisy, now-squirming Caroline. Stephanie Bolter looked at Anna's stomach, and so did Collin.

Anna sneaked her hand inside her shirt to quiet Caroline. But Caroline grabbed Anna's hand with her front claws and kicked it playfully with her back legs. The kicking hurt Anna. She wanted to scream and pull Caroline out of her shirt, but she could not. Stephanie and Collin were still staring at Anna's churning stomach. Anna grabbed Caroline's legs to hold her still, but Caroline did not want to be confined.

Mreeeew. Anna felt her face grow white.

Stephanie Bolter's hand flew into the air. "Miss Crystal," she called, "something's wrong with Anna. Her stomach is growling and she's holding it. I think she's going to be sick."

Miss Crystal looked at Anna. "Why, Anna, you do look pale," she said. "Aren't you feeling well?"

What could Anna do? What could she say? It would be very bad to lie to Miss Crystal. If she did, and if Miss Crystal found out, Miss Crystal would not trust Anna again. And it didn't seem that Anna could keep Caroline a secret any longer. Just then, Anna felt something warm and wet dribble down her skin. Caroline had gone to the bathroom inside Anna's shirt!

"Anna, why don't we walk to the sick room together," Miss Crystal said. Meekly, Anna followed Miss Crystal to the hall. She could feel Caroline churning inside her shirt, her feet sliding on Anna's wet skin. In the hall, Miss Crystal said, "Anna, what's the problem?"

While Anna was thinking about what she would say to Miss Crystal, she felt Caroline climb up the inside of her sweatshirt. She tried to block Caroline's way with her hand, but Caroline just squirmed around it until she poked her head out of the neck.

"Oh my!" said Miss Crystal to the tiny head. She pulled her out while Caroline squirmed and kicked like a miniature karate champion.

"What a frisky little thing," Miss Crystal said. "Well, Anna, we have a problem here, don't we?"

Anna was glad to hear Miss Crystal say "we" instead of "you."

"This little kitten doesn't seem to be ready for the third grade."

"No, Miss Crystal," Anna said.

Miss Crystal nodded to the wet spot on Anna's

sweatshirt. "You look a little damp, Anna. Let's clean you up first. Then we'll put your kitten in the teachers' lounge until it's time to go home. Shall we?"

Anna nodded, thankful to have a teacher like Miss Crystal. Many teachers would have been angry with Anna for bringing a cat to school. Many would have thought Anna was a nuisance and would have called Anna's parents. But not Miss Crystal. Gratefully, Anna walked with her to the teachers' lounge. Along the way, she got to tell the whole story to her teacher herself.

5

MINUTES

Kimberly had become more stuffed up each day. Now she was wheezing when she breathed. Anna *wanted* to believe Kimberly had a very bad cold. But Kimberly didn't have a fever or a sore throat. No. There was no avoiding the truth. Kimberly was allergic to Caroline. Anna had invited Bethie over to help her decide what to do.

In the hidey-hole, Bethie shone the flashlight on Anna's face. "Is this a real meeting, Anna, or are we just going to talk?" Bethie asked.

"It's a meeting," Anna said. Caroline stalked

Anna's foot, her rear end perched in the air, her tail switching. She pounced.

Because Anna and Bethie were having an official meeting, Anna wrote the "minutes" on a piece of paper. She wrote the date and the exact time: *4:11*. Anna figured that writing the minutes meant that you had to record the exact time. She wondered if you had to keep writing down the minutes for the whole report. To be safe, she would. By the time Anna had figured this out it was 4:12, so she wrote that on the paper.

Anna said, "Let's hurry up and start the meeting so I don't have to write so many minutes."

Now Caroline was stalking Bethie's foot. Anna was happy that Caroline had stalked her foot first, because that showed she liked Anna better. But she was happy Caroline was concentrating on Bethie now, because Bethie liked Caroline too.

"What's the meeting about?" Bethie asked.

"I saved Caroline from that awful hole and I really love her, but I don't think she can live here anymore." Anna's eyes grew wet with tears. "Kimberly's allergic. We have to think of a really good home for Caroline. That's what the meeting's for."

Bethie hugged her friend. "Oh, Anna, that's awful. You must feel terrible," she said. "I could take her, but Mom doesn't allow house cats. She'd just be a barn cat."

Bethie's family had a bunch of barn cats, and they were pretty wild and tough. "No, I don't think Caroline could be a barn cat," Anna said.

Bethie said, "Maybe my Uncle Larry in Hartford would take Caroline."

"Is Hartford near Door County?" Anna asked.

"Nope. It's near Milwaukee."

Anna wrote down *4:20.* "That's too far, Bethie. I'd like to visit Caroline, maybe every day. She'd miss me if she never saw me again." Then Anna added, "She'd miss you, too, Bethie. You helped save her, and I can tell she really likes you."

Bethie stroked Caroline's chin. "You're right, Anna. We need to find a home that's close enough to visit."

Anna wrote down *4:23. Bethie's uncle—NO.*

"How about Stephanie Bolter? They don't have any pets," suggested Bethie.

Anna said, "I think Stephanie likes to be the pet at her house. She wouldn't like to share the attention with a cute little kitten like Caroline.

Stephanie is such a priss!"

Anna knew it wasn't nice to call Stephanie a priss. But really, Stephanie *was* a priss, and Anna didn't think she'd make a very good owner anyway.

Bethie grinned. "You're right, Anna. Stephanie's selfish and wouldn't be very kind to Caroline."

Anna smiled back at her friend. A true friend understood about not liking prissy people. She was lucky to have such an understanding friend—especially when she had to give her kitten away. "So it's decided. We won't give Caroline to Stephanie."

"Right."

Anna wrote the new time: *4:28. Stephanie Bolter—NO!*

Anna rested her chin on her hand. She stared at Bethie. Anna had already thought and thought about what to do with Caroline. She was glad to give up thinking for a while and let Bethie figure it out. But Bethie was quiet too. Maybe she couldn't think of anyone either! The two friends huddled in the hidey-hole, trying to think of someone who could take Anna's kitten, while Caroline pranced around their feet.

"It has to be someone very nice," said Anna, recording *4:31*.

CAROLINE'S NEW OWNER
1. *Very nice*

"And someone who isn't allergic," Bethie said. "And someone whose Mother won't say no, or someone who doesn't have a mother."

"Wait a minute," Anna said. "I have to get this down." So she wrote:

4:36
2. *Not allergic*
3. *No mother problem*

"*Maybe*," said Bethie, "we could think of someone who already has pets. Then they would be nice and not allergic and everything else."

"Mrs. Sarafiny!" the girls whispered together.

Mrs. Sarafiny was perfect. She was kind and fun and brave, and she seemed prepared for anything. "Let's go see her now," Anna said.

Bethie looked at her watch. Long ago she had removed the plain metal band and tied it closed with ribbons to make it fancy. "It's already after four thirty. I have to get home to do chores," she said.

It would have been nice to give Caroline away

together. But Bethie's family was very large, and she had to help out. Anna put her arm around her friend. "It's okay," Anna said. "I can take Caroline myself."

Anna tucked Caroline inside her shirt again. Then she and Bethie left the hidey-hole. But Mom was in Anna's room, putting clean clothes away. She said, "Where are you girls going?"

Anna thought hard. She hadn't told Mom about Caroline, so she couldn't tell her about taking her to Mrs. Sarafiny now. But she didn't want to lie, either. What could she say?

Then Bethie said, "Home."

"Oh, that's fine. I'll see you later then, Anna." Of course, Mom thought that's where Anna was going too, and Anna let her think it. Anna and Bethie hurried downstairs. They were both blushing because of the half lie they had told. Anna felt bad that she'd misled Mom about where she was going, but she told herself she hadn't really lied—she had just not offered the truth. At least Anna was on the right track now. She and Bethie had decided on a home for Caroline. Soon Kimberly would be feeling better. Soon Anna would not be forced to hide the truth. Then Anna could concentrate on how to make Mom and Daddy happy with each other again. But, of course, everything depended on Mrs. Sarafiny taking Caroline.

Outside Anna held Caroline to her chest with her left hand and did the Best Friends Handshake with her right. She crossed her hand to her left shoulder, slapped her leg twice, snapped her fingers, and shook Bethie's hand. Then Bethie walked home and Anna walked up the big hill toward Mrs. Sarafiny's house.

It was a warm October day, warm enough for Anna to unzip her jacket. A fresh lake breeze pushed at the puffy clouds, forming them into cartoon animals. Anna would have liked to lie on Mrs. Sarafiny's hill and watch the sky. She would have liked to breathe in the lake air. But today wasn't a day for watching or breathing in. It was a day for giving away. As Anna walked, she kicked the little pebbles along the path. One got in the hole of her shoe and she had to bend down to pick it out. Caroline squirmed inside Anna's sweatshirt.

"We're almost there, Caroline. We're almost at your new home." Saying it made Anna feel sad, but she made her voice sound light and cheery, for Caroline. "You'll like it at Mrs. Sarafiny's. She's a very nice person and she has lots of other cats for you to play with."

Meeeew.

"I'll miss you too."

At last Anna was at the top of Cherrywood Hill. She noticed that Mrs. Sarafiny's grass was a little long. There were a lot of weeds growing in it. The paint was peeling on Mrs. Sarafiny's house, and all the inside shades were drawn. But there were cheery things there too. There were lots of birdhouses, some on poles, some nailed onto trees. And there were shutters with bumblebees painted on them!

Anna rang the bell. She saw one of the shades rise very slowly and Mrs. Sarafiny's fuzzy white head peer from beneath it. The shade snapped back down. "Why, Anna," cried Mrs. Sarafiny, flinging open the front door, "how nice to see you!" Mrs. Sarafiny's freckled cheeks were rosy red. She'd tied a little green ribbon into her flyaway hair.

Caroline peeped out of the top of Anna's jacket. "And you brought little Caroline with you! Come in! Come in!" Carefully, Anna took Caroline out of her jacket and put her in Mrs. Sarafiny's arms. Mrs. Sarafiny held Caroline to her chest and stroked her as she led Anna into the kitchen. Caroline nuzzled her head against Mrs. Sarafiny's chin. Good. If Caroline was really lovable, Mrs. Sarafiny couldn't refuse to take her. From every corner of the kitchen, eyes stared at Anna. Five pairs. The owner of one of them padded up to Anna and rubbed against her leg.

It was hot in Mrs. Sarafiny's kitchen, so Anna took off her jacket and folded it over the top of a kitchen chair. She took a minute to look around. Mrs. Sarafiny's kitchen was messy, a little like Anna's room. You could tell that Mrs. Sarafiny didn't like to throw things away. There were piles of old newspapers and magazines, and there was a whole counter full of empty cottage cheese cartons. Several cupboard doors were open. One was crammed full of folded pieces of aluminum foil.

"You've met all my darlings," Mrs. Sarafiny said to Anna, "but maybe you don't remember their names." Mrs. Sarafiny's blue eyes danced merrily. "This is Nancy," she said, nodding at the silvery Siamese who alternately purred and muttered to Anna from beneath the kitchen table. "Nancy is the most outgoing. She loves to talk, and she loves to make new friends."

A bulky black cat strode toward Anna. "This is Don, my big old tom. He's the leader of the pack, aren't you, big fella?" Mrs. Sarafiny crooned. She crouched down, with Caroline in her plump, freckled arms, as Don sniffed the kitten and then Anna. Anna guessed they passed inspection when Don plunked himself solidly on Anna's foot.

"Hi, Don," said Anna.

Mrs. Sarafiny's eyes turned toward the row of six food-and-water dishes. A sturdy little blond cat was eating at one of them. "That's Paul. Paul's always hungry, but he's a growing boy." Mrs. Sarafiny sighed.

"Hi, Paul," said Anna politely. Paul didn't look up from his food dish, though he did pause for a moment before snatching the next bite.

Mrs. Sarafiny nodded toward the shaded window. "Karen's the white Angora and Jenny's the little calico." Karen batted at the dangling shade pull. The pull was ragged and the paper shade was full of pinprick holes. Jenny was lying on the windowsill, her head hooked beneath the shade,

looking carefully at the other side. Mrs. Sarafiny bent toward Anna. "Jenny is the detective. She's always watching things, poking into things, figuring things out. My goodness, the things Jenny knows!"

"Hello, Jenny and Karen," said Anna. The kitchen seemed to be bursting with cats. Would there be room for Caroline?

Another cat walked in. This one was gray, with a neat white patch on his chest. He looked like he was wearing a gray suit and a white shirt. "John," said Mrs. Sarafiny simply. John was lean and had long, slender legs. John pounced on a kitchen chair and leaped to the tabletop. He settled on the newspaper. "I opened up the financial section for you, dear," Mrs. Sarafiny said to John. Then she said to Anna, "John likes to keep up with the business world." Strangely, Mrs. Sarafiny wasn't looking at Anna when she spoke to her. Her gaze was somewhere else. But when Anna turned to see what it was, there was nothing there.

"Oh my, oh my, oh my!" said Mrs. Sarafiny, suddenly clapping her forehead with her hand. Her plump little legs began to jerk forward as she walked toward the refrigerator. "Where are my manners? I'll bet you're thirsty!" she said to Anna.

"Yes, Mrs. Sarafiny, I am." Anna thought longingly about a big soda with plenty of ice cubes and maybe a maraschino cherry. Anna wasn't allowed to have soda at home before dinner. Mom said it was too sugary and full of empty calories. It would ruin Anna's appetite. But Anna was allowed to have soda at other people's homes.

Mrs. Sarafiny nodded eagerly, her fuzzy hair bouncing. "Good. I like to see a girl with a healthy appetite. I'll fix you some milk."

Darn it! Nutritious milk. "Okay," Anna said.

Mrs. Sarafiny opened the refrigerator and stood there, looking inside. Anna couldn't help noticing it was practically empty. There was only a small carton of milk, some mustard, and something in a plastic container. Anna had never seen a refrigerator as empty as this. Where was all of Mrs. Sarafiny's food? Was she too poor to buy it? But when she had rescued Anna, her bag had been full of food.

Anna said, "Mrs. Sarafiny, it doesn't look like you have very much food. I don't want to drink the last of your milk."

Mrs. Sarafiny turned around. She looked confused. "Milk?" she said. "Oh yes. Of course. That's what I was after. But don't be silly, Anna. You're welcome to the milk. I'm sure some more food will turn up somewhere."

Suddenly, Caroline bounded out of Mrs. Sarafiny's arms. She thumped to the floor and dashed over to the row of food dishes, skidding on the linoleum. Paul looked up for a minute, but then continued eating. Caroline nibbled from one food dish and then another, all the while moving closer and closer toward Paul.

Mrs. Sarafiny poured a mug full of milk for Anna. Anna thought it was strange to drink milk from a mug. Usually she drank milk out of a glass. But when Mrs. Sarafiny poured the milk into a little pan on the old white enamel stove, Anna thought she understood. "Are you fixing me cocoa?" she asked. Cocoa was one of Anna's favorite things. She especially liked to have it with Daddy after supper.

"No. I don't have chocolate. I'm just taking the chill off the milk. Cold milk isn't good for the digestive system."

Mrs. Sarafiny was fixing Anna warm milk!

Anna hated milk when it wasn't ice-cold. Warm milk tasted heavy and icky-sweet, but she didn't want to be rude, so she said, "Thank you."

Mrs. Sarafiny handed the warm mug of milk to Anna. Anna took a sip and choked it down, feeling the warmish milk slither slowly down her throat. By then, Caroline had worked her way to Paul's food dish. She began to nose into it and Paul nudged her gently away. Anna was worried. What if Paul became jealous and hurt Caroline? Caroline sneaked behind Paul and looked longingly at his tail. Oh no! Anna rushed to rescue Caroline just as she pounced on Paul's tail. There was a tumbling tangle of kittens and Anna couldn't grab on to Caroline. Anna stood back. Paul wasn't hurting Caroline! He was kicking her gently with his back feet and Caroline was nipping at his shoulder. They were playing!

"Look at those two!" exclaimed Mrs. Sarafiny, smiling widely. "Aren't they full of the old pizzazz? Paul needs a playmate. All the other cats are too old for him." Mrs. Sarafiny looked at Anna. "I'm glad you brought your kitten over."

Anna squeezed her eyes closed and gulped down a little more milk. She should say something to Mrs. Sarafiny now. But what if Mrs. Sarafiny wouldn't take Caroline? What would Anna do then? Anna felt like Mrs. Sarafiny was her last hope. If she didn't take Caroline, Anna would have to go home and explain the whole thing to her family. Anna took a deep breath and began. "Mrs. Sarafiny, Caroline is a wonderful kitten. She's cute and playful and sometimes she's very cuddly. But my sister, Kimberly, is allergic to her. I have to find Caroline a new home."

Immediately, Mrs. Sarafiny rushed to Caroline and plucked her up. "The little darling," she said.

Anna went on. "I was wondering . . . um . . . would you like to take Caroline?"

"Of course!" Mrs. Sarafiny said. Just like that.

Anna was surprised at how quickly Mrs. Sarafiny agreed. Anna had thought she'd have to talk her into it. She'd thought Mrs. Sarafiny would have to think it over carefully. Now Anna had many mixed-up feelings. At once she was re- lieved to have found a home for Caroline and sad that she was really, truly leaving. And something was strange about Mrs. Sarafiny and her house, something that made Anna uncomfortable.

"Do you mind if I visit Caroline?" asked Anna.

"Why no!" said Mrs. Sarafiny enthusiastically, her plump chest and fuzzy hair jiggling as she spoke. "Visit as often as you like."

Mrs. Sarafiny looked at the clock. "Oh my my my my!" she said. "It's almost five thirty. I have to lock up the house at five thirty precisely—I absolutely must!" She looked at Anna. "I'm afraid you'll have to go."

Anna wondered why. Why did she have to go? Why did Mrs. Sarafiny absolutely have to lock up the house at five thirty?

Anna picked up her jacket from the back of a kitchen chair. It was full of cat hair. In fact, little tufts of cat hair and dust bunnies were flying all around the kitchen. It made Anna's nose itch. Mrs. Sarafiny was a pretty sloppy housekeeper.

Before Anna left, she picked up Caroline and scratched the very soft, very fuzzy part under her chin. Caroline raised her chin in appreciation and purred. How Anna would miss her little kitten! Gently, Anna put Caroline down. She turned quickly so Mrs. Sarafiny wouldn't see her eyes fill with tears. "Good-bye," she said, opening the door. "Good-bye."

Anna closed the door behind her. She didn't

look back. She didn't see Mrs. Sarafiny hold Caroline up to the window and help her wave good-bye with her little gray paw. Anna walked toward home. It was almost dark. There were no other houses on Mrs. Sarafiny's hill. So Anna felt she could cry now because no one would hear. Hot tears trickled down her cheeks. She sat on the ground and hugged her knees as she cried. Anna hadn't realized how hard it would be to say good-bye to Caroline.

Slowly, when her tears stopped, Anna sniffed noisily. She turned off the pebble path on Mrs. Sarafiny's hill and walked to Prairie View Court. When she got home, the last thing Anna wanted to hear was silence. But inside, Anna's house was quiet, as if no one were home. Yet there was Daddy reading the paper, and Mom reading a book, and Kimberly doing her homework. It made Anna nervous to have everyone so silent. This was just before dinner. At this time, Anna's family was usually noisy and busy. They would be talking and singing, and the radio would be on. They would be making dinner, setting the table, and talking about their day. What was going on?

"Hello, Anna," Daddy said, snapping his newspaper down and looking at his daughter with a serious face. At first, Anna was worried that everybody was angry with her. Had they found out about Caroline? But soon Anna realized Daddy didn't have a you're-in-big-trouble-young-lady look on his face. He wasn't angry at Anna. Daddy announced, "Anna's home. Perhaps dinner should be started." But Daddy wasn't talking to Mom. He was talking to the air, to no one in particular.

Mom continued to look at her book as she said, "I can see perfectly well that Anna is home. Perhaps if Someone wants dinner, Someone can start it." Mom wasn't talking to Daddy either. She was talking to the air too!

Oh no! Oh no! Mom and Daddy were having another fight. Only this was worse than a fight. This was *silence*. Anna ran to her room. She didn't want to see Mom and Daddy like this. Anna threw herself on her bed. She held on to Small Bear, the little bear that had been hers since she was three. Anna rocked back and forth, Small Bear in her arms. It wasn't fair! Anna felt like she was too full of sadness. Already, she had been sad about giving up Caroline. She'd been worried, too, about Mrs. Sarafiny. More than ever, she had needed a happy, loving family. Instead, Mom and Daddy were fighting again! Would they ever stop?

Soon Kimberly burst into the room. She sat next to Anna on Anna's bed. The sisters looked at each other for a while, each with moist, worried faces. Kimberly picked at the fuzzy tufts on Anna's bedspread and began to cry. "Mom and Daddy are fighting," she cried. "And I'm so worried! I hate it when they fight!" Kimberly plucked a whole fuzzy tuft right out of Anna's bedspread. Now the spot was bald.

Anna wrapped her thin arms around her sister. "Me too," Anna said. "I hate it so much." Anna wanted to say something to comfort Kimberly, but Anna herself felt cold and empty inside. How could she comfort Kimberly when she felt so sad? Anna swallowed the lump in her throat. It would make Kimberly feel worse to see Anna cry too. But the lump wouldn't go down. It filled Anna's throat and it felt like it was going to choke her. Soon Anna was crying too. Anna and Kimberly held on to each other until the tears stopped.

When they walked downstairs, Mom was filling a big pot with hot water. There was a jar of spaghetti sauce on the counter. Daddy was making salad.

Had Mom and Daddy made up? Anna searched their faces for a sign. Mom's face was smooth, not ridged and white like it had been before. Daddy was smiling. They had made up. The fight was over! Now everything would be back to normal! Now they loved each other again!

Anna looked at Kimberly and Kimberly smiled at her. Even Kimberly's allergies were over!

Anna rushed up to Daddy and threw her arms around his long legs. "Anna!" he said. Daddy picked up his little girl—his Anna!—and sat her on the counter. Anna used to sit on the counter when she was a little girl. How she loved to watch Mom and Daddy from this high-up spot. Tenderly, Daddy wrapped his arms around Anna and held her tight. Anna plunged her nose into the spot she liked best, the part between Daddy's collar and his neck. More than anything, Anna loved that smell. It was a little bit of laundry soap, newspaper smell, and Daddy. Anna never, never wanted to let go.

6

SATURDAY CHORES

Anna missed Caroline's warm little body against her leg. She missed carrying her around in her shirt. She missed Caroline's tiny voice and her pointy tail and her kitten smile. Anna even missed having Caroline pounce on her bare feet and dig her sharp, slivery claws into her skin. Clawing hurt, of course, but hurting was part of being a pet owner. But missing Caroline hurt too much! Anna didn't feel she could last another day without seeing her dear little kitten again.

Today was Saturday. Anna had to do a few

chores at home, and then she could go to the Adventure Club meeting at ten o'clock. She was going to meet Bethie in the Hendersons' cow tunnel. Anna wanted today's adventure to be a visit to Mrs. Sarafiny and Caroline. She was sure Bethie wouldn't mind.

"Anna," called Mom from downstairs, "I have your chores ready."

Anna took her time getting downstairs, where Mom and Kimberly were waiting. Anna wasn't happy to see Mom holding her red Wisconsin Badgers hat with too many slips of yellow paper inside. Sometimes, when Mom had *lots* of chores, she wrote each one on a little piece of paper. She put things like "fifteen minutes of free reading" on the papers too, to make it seem more like a game.

"Okay, girls," said Mom brightly, "let's see what each of you picks. Kimberly first." Mom shook up the hat and the papers bounced around like popcorn. Too bad they weren't.

Kimberly caught one of the papers from the bouncing bunch and read, "'Water plants.' Good. I like to do that."

Anna didn't *mind* watering the plants, but she didn't like it either. It didn't really seem natural

96

for a kid to like doing a job, even if it was watering the plants. Anna picked next. "'Do breakfast dishes.' Ugh," she said, "that's such a big one!" Kimberly's face looked sorry, and it made Anna angry. She hated it more when Kimberly felt sorry for her!

Kimberly picked next. "Yay! I got 'fifteen minutes of free reading.'"

Lucky duck. Anna hoped there were two more free-reading papers in the hat and that she would get them. She was in a big hurry to finish so she could get to Mr. Henderson's cow tunnel. If she got two free readings, she could do them later. But in the end, the lists looked like this:

KIMBERLY

water plants
fifteen minutes of free reading
take newspapers in wagon to Ivy Hallam's
fifteen minutes of free reading

ANNA

do breakfast dishes
sweep front porch
vacuum inside of car
fold load of laundry

Anna was usually luckier than this. Usually she got at least one free reading and two easy jobs. This time Kimberly got all the easy ones *and* the reading. It wasn't fair!

"Oh, Anna," Kimberly said sorrowfully when she looked at Anna's list. "You got all the hard jobs and I got all the easy ones."

"Yeah," Anna said, frowning.

"Tell you what. I'll switch with you. I'll give you my free reading and watering the plants and take your doing the dishes and vacuuming the car."

Then Kimberly's list would be worse than Anna's. Maybe Kimberly hadn't figured that out. Should Anna tell her? But no, Kimberly probably knew. She was probably being generous. The thought of generous Kimberly made the dough-nuts from breakfast churn around inside Anna's stomach. Should she refuse Kimberly's offer? Maybe Anna should even offer to do an extra job of Kimberly's. Then she would look very grown-up and responsible. Mom and Kimberly would be impressed. But Daddy and Mom were getting along better now, and it didn't seem so important to be *so* good. Surely Anna could afford to take it easy for just one day and accept Kimberly's offer.

Besides, Caroline probably missed Anna. It was for Caroline's sake that Anna finally said, "I'd like to switch. Thanks."

It took Anna about an hour to finish her chores. It was late, and she had to run all the way to Mr. Henderson's. Mr. Henderson's cows were standing around on the hilly pasture, next to the cow tunnel. They looked up at Anna with large, patient eyes. "Hi, girls!" Anna yelled to them. Then she ran down the hill to the tunnel.

"Bethie!" Anna cried, out of breath.

"Anna!" cried Bethie, her call echoing from inside the cement tunnel.

Anna ran inside. She liked the way her shoes made loud, clapping sounds from inside the big tunnel. "HEY!" she yelled, just so she could hear the thunderous, echoing noise.

"YA!" yelled Bethie, because she liked to hear the echo too.

They yelled for a little while. Mr. Henderson's cows were startled, and began to leap and run from the noise. The stiff, bulky cows jerked into the air, landing heavily on their bulgy-kneed legs. When they ran, their pink udders swung from side to side. There was nothing funnier than

a big, clumsy cow jumping around a pasture.

Just then, Mr. Henderson's head appeared at the other end of the tunnel. Bethie and Anna drew in a quick breath.

"What are you girls doing here?" Mr. Henderson asked. The echo of his voice hung in the air.

Bethie and Anna each waited for the other to answer. Finally Bethie said, "We're . . . uh . . . part of a club. The Adventure Club. We meet here to plan our adventures."

"But we go someplace else for our adventures," Anna quickly added. "We don't snoop around here or anything."

"And we don't do anything bad."

Mr. Henderson chuckled a deep, throaty laugh. It sounded loose and full, and it made Anna like him at once. "An Adventure Club, eh? Right here in the cow tunnel?"

Anna began, "Yes . . ."

". . . Sir," Bethie added, making sure to be polite.

"Well, I suppose it gives the girls something to talk about over there." Mr. Henderson nodded at the black-and-white cows peacefully chewing grass. "They like a bit of excitement." Mr.

101

Henderson's face was brown and cracked, like dried-up dirt. His lips were thin and his smile was wide.

Anna felt this was a good time to ask, now that Mr. Henderson was all chuckly, "So you don't mind if we have our meetings here?"

"Nope. But try to keep it down. The cows get jumpy when you shout. Can you do that?"

"Sure," Bethie said.

"Thank you, ladies." Mr. Henderson tipped his hat. "Well, 'bye, then."

As he left, Anna called out, "Mr. Henderson, you can be an honorary member of our Adventure Club."

Mr. Henderson turned and looked at the girls. "I'd like that."

After Mr. Henderson left, Bethie said, "Let's make the Wisconsin dairy cow our official mascot."

"Great!" said Anna. Then she added, "Bethie, I know it's your turn for an adventure, but there's something special I'd like to do. I really miss Caroline, and it would be fun to visit her and Mrs. Sarafiny."

Bethie looked down. "I can't."

"What?"

Bethie looked uneasy. "Mom hit the roof this morning. She walked into my room. . . . You know my room is a little messy."

"A little," Anna said diplomatically. The truth was, you couldn't walk a step or sit down anywhere in Bethie's room because of all the stuff. Anna's side of her room wasn't exactly *neat,* but it was hospital clean compared to Bethie's.

"Anyway, Mom said, 'Young lady, I don't want you to do a single thing until this room is spotless.'" Bethie waggled her finger to imitate her mother. "'This is a dump. It's a disaster area. Get to it.'"

Anna shook her head sadly, in sympathy for her friend. "I hate it when parents call us 'young ladies.' It always means trouble or work."

"I know." Bethie sucked in her lower lip. "But that means I won't be able to visit Caroline with you. I had to practically beg her to let me come here before cleaning my room."

"Could you come later?" Anna asked.

"It's going to take me all day to clean my room. It's pretty bad," Bethie admitted.

Anna felt herself grow older as she made this generous offer. "I can help."

Bethie's eyes widened. "You'll help me *clean my room?*"

Anna nodded. "Yes. Then, when we're done we can visit Caroline."

"Anna, you are a truer friend than anyone. True blue."

Anna smiled.

"Race you home," Bethie said, and the two girls started running out of the tunnel.

Bethie's house was comfortable, like a favorite tennis shoe, and Anna loved it. It seemed as though noise came out of every corner, bounced off of every wall. Anna loved her own house—it was cozy and neat and full of books and music. But Bethie's house was like an amusement park. The inside always smelled good, like food cooking. There were people and animals all over. Bethie's family raised German shepherds, so there was a noisy, friendly kennel in the back. And then there was a barn full of cats—always new ones with each litter. And as much as Bethie said her six big brothers were a pain, you could tell she really liked them.

When Bethie and Anna walked inside, Seth, two brothers up from Bethie, said, "Wooo-ooo,

Bethie. You're in deep trouble. I heard Mom call you 'young lady.' What did you do?"

"Her room's a disaster area," yelled Rob, from the porch. Rob was scooping up dog food to take to the kennel. "Mom said she has to clean it . . . or else!"

Seth grabbed his stomach as though he'd been shot with a cannon. "Oh no!" He fell to the sagging brown sofa as he said, "You're dead meat, Bethie. You'll never get that room clean."

"See if I won't," said Bethie, crisply. "Anna's going to help."

Anna and Bethie walked up the stairs and into Bethie's room. Both stood there, gaping at the accumulated stuff. They didn't know where to start. Soon the door creaked open and a thick rope was tossed inside. Seth's voice said, "Here, Anna. If you get stuck in Bethie's garbage, use this to pull yourself out."

"Seth, you pig," Bethie yelled, throwing the rope back at Seth and rolling her eyes at Anna.

Seth called from the other side. "Listen. If you don't come out in an hour, I'll call 911 to rescue you."

"Pig," yelled Bethie.

"Slob," yelled Seth.

How Anna would love to have a big brother to yell at instead of Generous Kimberly.

There were toys and tapes in Bethie's room, balls and books. There was a Frisbee with gobs of melted candy on it. There were zillions of school papers and old lunch bags and slimy-looking things. Anna didn't even want to think about what the slimy-looking things were. It took a long, long time to clean Bethie's room. It took the rest of the morning.

Then Bethie's mom poked her head into the room. Bethie's mom was a red-cheeked woman with the same root-beer eyes as Bethie's. She had short jet-black hair, and she generally wore jeans and a loose shirt. Anna knew Bethie's mom worked in a lab. She figured it must be fun to do things with microscopes all day.

"Why, Bethie! You've got a room you can be proud of again. Congratulations!" Bethie's mom's eyes were full of snap and sparkle.

Seth butted his head in too. "Hey, Elizabeth," he said, shaking his head in disbelief. "What did you use—a bulldozer? A gang of garbage men?"

Just then, the noon whistle blew. "It's lunchtime," said Bethie's mother. "Anna, would you like to join us?"

"Sure," Anna said.

Bethie's mom smiled. "Good. I'll call your mother to tell her where you are. Lunch will be ready in a sec."

Anna, Bethie, Bethie's mom, and Seth trooped down the stairs. Bethie kept jabbing at Seth till they got to the kitchen.

After lunch, Anna and Bethie ran all the way to Mrs. Sarafiny's. Anna rang the bell. They had to wait a long time before they saw Mrs. Sarafiny's white fuzzy head peek beneath the window shade. She opened the door just a tiny crack. "Oh!" she said. "Anna and Bethie! I'll let you inside in just a minute, but you must look carefully behind you. You can never be too sure you aren't being followed."

Followed? Who would follow Bethie and Anna? Bethie looked behind her. "Nobody's there," she said.

"Look in the air," Mrs. Sarafiny said. "Sometimes they're in the air."

Anna wasn't sure who "they" were and she wasn't sure where "in the air" was. Did Mrs. Sarafiny mean the sky? Did she mean the air around their heads? So Anna looked around her. "No. Nothing is in the air."

Mrs. Sarafiny opened the door reluctantly and let them in. "Well, you can never be too sure," she said.

"How's Caroline?" Anna asked.

"See for yourself," Mrs. Sarafiny said, reaching behind a big green plant. The plant was shaking, and Anna saw why. Caroline had wrapped her front paws around the stem and was pummeling the poor plant with her back feet. Mrs. Sarafiny plucked the feisty little kitten out from the plant. Eagerly, Anna reached out her arms.

How warm Caroline felt! Anna nestled her nose into Caroline's fur. She smelled so good! Caroline purred as Anna flicked little bits of torn plant from her fur.

"Oh, Anna," Bethie said, "look how happy Caroline is to see you!"

Anna nodded, too full of happiness to speak. "Can you stay for a while?" Mrs. Sarafiny asked Bethie and Anna.

"Sure," Bethie said.

"How about a game of canasta?" Mrs. Sarafiny asked, grinning.

"Is that a board game or cards?" Anna asked.

"Cards. I guess that means you don't know how to play. Well," Mrs. Sarafiny said briskly, "it's high time you learned." Mrs. Sarafiny opened a drawer and rummaged around inside. Other people's drawers were always interesting, so Anna got close enough to look. There were bits of tin foil and rubber bands and peanut shells in there. It looked a lot like Bethie's room. Soon Mrs. Sarafiny found the cards. "Here they are," she said. "And here's the automatic shuffler."

Mrs. Sarafiny nudged John and the financial section off the table. The newspaper was pretty yellow, so Anna looked at the date. It was a month old. Anna wondered if John realized he was reading old financial news.

"Okay," Mrs. Sarafiny said. "I'll go over a few of the rules and then we can start to play."

Mrs. Sarafiny divided the deck in two and placed them in the card shuffler. She cranked it and the cards miraculously fell into place.

"Can I do that?" Anna asked.

"Sure."

Anna held Caroline on her lap and cranked while Mrs. Sarafiny explained the rules. "First, jokers are wild. We play with a double deck, which is why I have a card shuffler. I've had it twenty-five years. Or is it thirty? Anyway, canasta is 500 points. Oh. Deuces are wild too."

"What are deuces?" Bethie asked.

"Twos. They're wild. Now, if you pick up the discard pile, you have to take all the cards. I think that's it. You can add to your meld any-time."

Anna hadn't heard anything quite so compli-cated since someone tried to explain long division to her. She thought she could live her whole life quite happily without either long division or this game. But maybe it was the way Mrs. Sarafiny was explaining it. She kept jumping around, say-ing things that didn't go together.

Somehow the three friends began to play. The game didn't go very smoothly, and Mrs. Sarafiny kept changing her mind about the rules. But they muddled through. When they were done, Mrs. Sarafiny said, "Who's hungry?"

Anna was surprised to realize she was, even though she'd eaten at Bethie's. "I am," she said, but hoped Mrs. Sarafiny wouldn't give her warm milk again.

Mrs. Sarafiny got up and stretched. With Anna following, she walked over to the refrigerator and opened it. But there was nothing inside! Not even milk. Mrs. Sarafiny stood at the refrigerator a long time, her face screwed up with confusion. "Well, I guess I can't give you anything. All I have is cat food."

Was Mrs. Sarafiny very poor? That didn't seem right, because she had had liver and candy bars when she had saved Bethie and Anna from the hole. Where was her food now?

"If you don't have any food, you must be hungry," Anna said.

"Now that you mention it, I am. Can't think of the last time I ate a real meal. The cats share their food, though."

Mrs. Sarafiny ate cat food? Anna thought that was the most disgusting thing she'd ever heard. Her heart went out to her new friend. Whatever the reason, it was awful for a person to be hungry.

Even worse to have to eat cat food.

"I guess you have to go grocery shopping," Bethie suggested.

"Well, that's surely true. But I can't, for the life of me, figure out where all the food went." Suddenly Mrs. Sarafiny slammed the door shut. "Why, it's the bad ones, the Martians. They're always trying to get me, get into my head, and now they've come into this house and stolen all my food. I tell you, those Martians are the biggest threat to our country." Mrs. Sarafiny's eyes narrowed. That made her look funny. "I've tried to warn people. I've written our governor and the president, but as far as I know, they haven't done a thing. All we citizens can do now is watch out for ourselves."

Caroline jumped from Anna's arms. Anna felt like jumping too, and running far far away. This was just too weird. It scared Anna to have a grown-up act so strange. Grown-ups should be predictable. You should be able to guess what they'd do. When a grown-up acted weird, you just never knew. Anna remembered when she was afraid of the ocean. She saw the waves come up and crash on the beach, and she was never sure just how far they'd go. So she wouldn't play in the sand. Anna felt that way about Mrs. Sarafiny now. How far would she go? How strange would she get?

Anna felt bad for Mrs. Sarafiny. Anna didn't believe about the Martians, but Mrs. Sarafiny did. That must be why she kept her shades drawn and thought Anna and Bethie were being followed by the Martians. The fact that she didn't have food and ate *cat food* proved she needed some kind of help.

But Anna was only nine years old. Mrs. Sarafiny needed her family at a time like this. Where were they? She was *Mrs.* Sarafiny, after all, so that meant she was married to somebody, and maybe even had grown children or other relatives. But Mrs. Sarafiny was starving right now! She couldn't wait for Anna to tell her family. Anna had to find a quick way to get food to her. The only problem was that Mom and Daddy didn't know she was friends with Mrs. Sarafiny. They would probably be mad at her if they knew. So what could she do?

Well, Anna had to do something! Mrs. Sarafiny had helped Anna; now Anna would help her.

7

ALUMINUM FOIL?

Anna and Bethie met in the cow tunnel to discuss their rescue plans. Anna sat on the bottom curve of the tunnel and propped her feet on the sides. She held a notebook and pen in her hand. The pen had a little cow on the tip, instead of an eraser, now that the Wisconsin dairy cow was the Adventure Club's official mascot. She wrote the date and the time, 12:04, on the top of the paper.

"The most important thing is food. We have to get food to Mrs. Sarafiny right away," Bethie said.

Anna wrote *12:06* and *food* on her paper and

underlined "food" twice. "Right. I have sixteen dollars and fifty-three cents in my money jar. I used to have more, but I just bought a card shuffler like Mrs. Sarafiny's."

Bethie tucked her hair behind her ear. "Well, we can buy pretty much with sixteen dollars. Plus I have about twenty-three dollars."

Anna put down the new time—*12:08*—and added up the numbers in her notebook. "That makes thirty-nine dollars." Then she had an idea. "We can get some food from home, too. I'll tell Mom I'm collecting for the poor, which is true. Mom always gives food to the poor."

"I'll say the same thing to my mom. Let's get the food and meet back here. Then we can take it to Mrs. Sarafiny's."

"I think we should find out about Mrs. Sarafiny's family, too," Anna said. "Maybe there's somebody who can help her."

"Yes," Bethie agreed.

Anna wrote down the last minute, 12:15, and sighed deeply. What could be more rewarding than helping a starving friend? Besides, it was Sunday, church day, and Anna felt that today she would be doubly blessed for her charity.

All the way home, Anna glowed with warmth and goodwill. She imagined how grateful Mrs. Sarafiny would be when she got the groceries. She imagined how hungry she must feel now, and how good she'd feel after she had enough to eat. Kimberly had done many things in her life, but she had never rescued a starving person. The only problem was, Anna wouldn't be able to tell anyone about her good deed, because then her parents would find out about Caroline. Anna thought: I'll spend *all my money* and rescue a starving person, and still no one will know about it. But that's the way it is with generous people.

Anna swung open the front door and let it bang against the wall. "I'm home," she yelled. It was a sunny October day, and Daddy was outside in the hammock, reading the Sunday paper. Kimberly was doing her homework. Mom was in the kitchen—baking apple pie! It smelled so warm and cinnamony. How sad that Mrs. Sarafiny didn't have a mother like Anna's to bake her pies.

"Mom," Anna said, "I forgot to tell you. I need to collect food for the poor."

"Oh?" Mom said. She rolled out the leftover

pie dough into a circle. "A food drive. Well, we certainly have plenty of food, and I'm grateful for that. The least we can do is help people who don't have as much. Help yourself, Anna."

Anna looked at the leftover pie dough. "Are those going to be pinwheels?" she asked.

"Yes. Would you like to brush on the butter?"

Anna rushed to the stove, where a little pan of melted butter was waiting on a burner. She carried it to the pie dough and brushed it on. She wrote ANNA with her finger in the melted butter.

"Here's the cinnamon and sugar," Mom said, handing Anna a fragrant dish. Anna sprinkled that on top. Mom rolled the dough together. While she cut out the little pinwheels with a knife, Anna went into the pantry. She decided that Mrs. Sarafiny was most in need of the nutritious things that Anna didn't happen to like. So peas, sauerkraut, tomato soup, and vegetable juice went into Anna's paper bag. After all, how many times had Mom tried to get Anna to eat those things by telling her how good they were for her? Yes. Those nutritious things were perfect to give to Mrs. Sarafiny.

Anna got her money from the jar in her room.

She had stashed the jar behind *A Young Lady's Treasury of Poetry*, a thick book she didn't particularly care for. She always felt her money was safe there, because she didn't think anyone else would pull out that book either. The dollar bills were all squished inside the jar, and Anna had to pry them loose. The jar looked very empty without the $16.53, so Anna tried not to look at it. For a minute she thought about putting half the money back. It might be good to have something in case a real emergency came up. But then Anna decided that this *was* a real emergency. She put all the money in her pocket and lifted the paper bag full of food. She rushed to the cow tunnel, her change bouncing in her pocket, the cans in her bag getting heavier by the minute. "I got some good stuff," she yelled, running down the hill.

"Me too," Bethie yelled back.

Inside the tunnel, they looked at each other's treasures. Everything was vegetables. "Well," Bethie said, "vegetables *are* good for you. They're probably just the thing for Mrs. Sarafiny to eat."

But now Anna wasn't so sure. She thought about how yummy the apple pie smelled. "All vegetables sounds so boring."

"Yeah. Let's drop these things off at Mrs. Sarafiny's now. Then we can go shopping and buy her some fun things to eat."

"I think that's a wise idea," Anna said, nodding thoughtfully. Being generous made Anna feel older, and saying "wise idea" sounded especially grown-up.

Anna and Bethie went to Mrs. Sarafiny's and rang the doorbell. They rang again. Why didn't she answer the door? Anna began to worry that something had happened to her. When Anna heard a long tearing sound, she really began to worry. She rang the doorbell again. She let her breath out in a sudden *whoosh* when she saw Mrs. Sarafiny's white head peep underneath the window shade. She opened the door a little and looked at the girls. There was something funny on Mrs. Sarafiny's head! What was it?

"Come in! Come in!" Mrs. Sarafiny said nervously. "You shouldn't be out there like that. The Martians are too dangerous. The house is protected now, so you'll be safe in here."

Bethie and Anna exchanged worried glances.

"No," Bethie said, "we don't have time to stay. We just came to drop this off. My Mom was cleaning out her cupboards and she was just going to throw this food away. I thought you might like it, since you haven't had time to go grocery shopping yet."

Mrs. Sarafiny smiled. But her eyes darted nervously back and forth. Anna figured she was watching out for the Martians. "Why, isn't that nice!"

Anna and Bethie smiled. It felt so good to help someone. Anna shoved her bag toward Mrs. Sarafiny, who was still on the other side of the door. "Can you take this?" she asked. "Then we'll go and get the rest."

Anna recognized Caroline's nose against the crack of the door. "Sure thing," said Mrs. Sarafiny. "Just leave the bags there and I'll pick them up later . . . and thanks!" Caroline moved away and Mrs. Sarafiny closed the door.

As soon as Bethie and Anna were out of earshot, they began to discuss what they had seen. "What was Mrs. Sarafiny wearing on her head?" Bethie asked.

"I think it was a shower cap."

"You're right! But what was that silver stuff inside the hat?"

"It looked like aluminum foil."

Bethie stopped. She had a very curious look on her face. "Why did she line her shower cap with aluminum foil?"

Anna was stumped. "I don't know," she said. "It's pretty weird."

When they got to Doubleday's Grocery, Anna whisked a cart from the line. She pushed it with one foot on the rung and hopped along with the other.

"What should we get?" Bethie asked.

"Hot dogs and peanut butter," Anna said. "They're nutritious and good." Bethie put hot dogs in the cart. On the way to pick up the peanut butter, they passed a display of cheese. They decided on the squirt-out kind because it was so much fun to use. Then they put in bread, peanut butter, jelly, canned peaches, and chocolate syrup.

"Now we have to get some fun things," Anna said.

"Corn chips, for sure," said Bethie, piling a few

bags into the cart. "They go with the squirting cheese."

"And we know Mrs. Sarafiny likes candy bars. Remember when she had them the night she rescued us?" Anna felt that returning the favor of candy bars was an especially right thing to do. They put several in the cart.

"And something for luck," said Anna, "because Mrs. Sarafiny could really use some good luck."

"Fortune cookies!" suggested Bethie. Fortune cookies went into the shopping cart too.

"I hope we have enough money," Anna said.

"If we don't, we can take back the hot dogs," Bethie said.

Bethie and Anna stood in line to pay for the food. Anna noticed several paperback books on the display. She'd often thought of becoming a famous author when she grew up. She thought now that her experience with Mrs. Sarafiny would make a good story. Maybe it would win an award and Anna would appear on television. Anna wouldn't tell Mom and Daddy about Mrs. Sarafiny and Caroline until the show. Then she'd reveal that she was really the girl in the story on television. Of course, Mom and Daddy would be surprised. But by then, they wouldn't be angry at Anna anymore. Instead, they would be proud that their daughter was both a famous author *and* a generous person.

"Thirty-two dollars and fourteen cents," said a bored voice. Anna looked at the not-very-happy face of the check-out clerk. The clerk's face looked like it had been carved out of wood. Her eyes were glazed, like the glass eyes of a stuffed animal. Anna and Bethie quickly paid for the food and walked out of the store. Anna was happy she was going to be a famous author and not a check-out clerk. That didn't look like a very fun job.

Anna and Bethie carried their gifts to Mrs. Sarafiny. This time she was waiting for them. She opened the door just a crack. "Hurry in! Hurry in," she said, motioning with her hand, her eyes searching the air all the while.

Anna and Bethie squeezed inside. Then they stood, stock-still, as if they were planted. Their mouths dropped open and their eyes grew wide. *The entire kitchen was wallpapered with aluminum foil!* Even the windows. That's why it had taken Mrs. Sarafiny so long to open the window shade earlier this afternoon—she'd had to loosen the foil. The ripping sound that had worried Anna must have been the masking tape that Mrs. Sarafiny used to fasten the foil. Why did Mrs. Sarafiny cover her kitchen this way?

And Mrs. Sarafiny herself looked worried. She was wearing the same dress she'd worn the day before and paper hospital slippers. Her hair was more flyaway than usual, and on her head was the shower cap Anna and Bethie had noticed earlier. Like the kitchen, it was lined in aluminum foil.

"We brought you some more food, Mrs. Sarafiny," Anna said, holding out the paper bag of groceries.

Mrs. Sarafiny was holding Caroline, patting her gently. Her eyes filled with tears. "Why, isn't that sweet?" she said. "You know, I think it's been a long time since I've had people food." She straightened up a bit as she said, "Of course, I haven't starved or anything. You'd be surprised how tasty cat food is when it's warmed up a bit."

Anna shifted uneasily. She hated to hear about Mrs. Sarafiny eating cat food. It made her feel so sad.

Finally, Bethie asked the thing that was bothering them both. "Mrs. Sarafiny, why are the walls papered with aluminum foil?"

Mrs. Sarafiny laughed merrily as Caroline squirmed out of her arms. "Isn't it clever? I wondered, at first, how the Martians got in here to steal my food." She tapped her forehead with a finger. "But I'm a smart cookie and I figured it out. They send rays in here. They beamed my food up with rays. They can even overhear our conversation or beam instructions down to me with those rays. I hear them talking all the time." Mrs. Sarafiny snapped her fingers. "But I haven't heard a peep out of them since I papered the walls with foil. It bounces the rays off, don't you see? So now it's perfectly safe in here."

Oh no! thought Anna. Mrs. Sarafiny was more than hungry and a little worried. She was crazy! She really was! It made Anna nervous to see a grown-up acting so weird, but she was determined to stay and help her. She had to find out right away if there was a relative who could help Mrs. Sarafiny.

"Mrs. Sarafiny," she began, "do you have a husband?"

"Ernie? God rest his soul, he's gone more than

126

a year. Or is it five? Well, I'm not sure anymore."

Bethie said, "Do you have children?"

Mrs. Sarafiny shook her head sadly. She picked up John, the financial cat. "These are my children." Mrs. Sarafiny kissed John tenderly on the nose and he purred loudly. "Ernie and I never had babies, though we sure would have liked them. But then the cats started coming. They came right to my door, you see, all of them. And I've taken good care of them," Mrs. Sarafiny said, looking at John, "haven't I, babies?"

Bethie sighed deeply. Her face showed she was as worried about Mrs. Sarafiny as Anna was. No husband and no children. It didn't sound very good, so far.

"But you must have other relatives. Maybe a sister," suggested Anna, thinking about how much Kimberly would like to help poor Anna if she were in a fix like Mrs. Sarafiny.

"Nobody. I had a brother, but he died. No. It's just me and the kitties."

Mrs. Sarafiny, all alone! How awful that would be! Then, because Anna sensed Mrs. Sarafiny's deep sadness and loneliness, she wrapped her arms around her friend and held her tight. Soon

127

she felt Bethie's arms around Mrs. Sarafiny too. The three clung together for a long time, each one comforting the other.

"Now you have Bethie and me, too," Anna said.

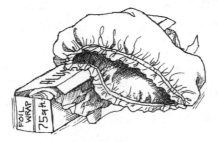

8

TV DINNER

After Bethie and Anna left Mrs. Sarafiny, they hadn't been able to say anything to each other. Anna felt numb. She didn't know what to think. She didn't know what to do. Anna had a hard time getting to sleep that night. She tossed and turned, her legs churning like an eggbeater under the covers. Anna stared out the window, her covers kicked into a tangle at her feet, but the pale moon offered no comfort tonight.

Anna was pretty sure Mrs. Sarafiny was crazy.

She thought the Martians were out to get her. She thought they beamed her food up and talked to her and listened to her conversations. That was crazy. Papering the kitchen with aluminum foil was crazy too. And not eating, not going outside, being afraid and alone, were not good for Mrs. Sarafiny, either. Anna and Bethie would have to keep a careful eye on their friend.

The next morning Anna woke up anxious to talk to Bethie about Mrs. Sarafiny. But Bethie wasn't on the bus. She wasn't at school, either. Was Bethie sick? The class was already seated when Bethie rushed into the class-room.

"I'm sorry, Miss Crystal. The alarm clock didn't go off and we overslept. Dad had to drive us to school."

"That's fine, Bethie. I'm glad you got here," said Miss Crystal.

Bethie heaved her backpack down, dug around in her desk, and pulled out a piece of paper and a pencil. She began to write. Soon Collin nudged Anna. He passed her a note from Bethie. It said:

Anna,

What do you think is wrong with Mrs. Sarafiny?

Best Friends Forever,
Bethie

Anna wrote back:

Bethie,

I'm pretty sure she's crazy. What do you know about crazy people?

B.F.F.,
Anna

Miss Crystal flipped the lights off and on. That signal meant she was going to make an announcement. "Class," she said, walking to the front of the room, "we're going to have our health test now. I'll pass out the papers. You'll have fifteen minutes to work."

Miss Crystal handed Anna her test. Anna flipped through the pages. There were three. She looked at a few of the questions. They were pretty easy, but then, health was always easy. You learned in the first grade about brushing teeth and bathing and washing your hair. After that, there wasn't any new information anyway. Anna would have no problem finishing the test in fifteen minutes, so she let herself drift off for just a little while.

What if Mrs. Sarafiny got worse? What would Anna do then? She was only nine years old. She couldn't get more money to buy food. She couldn't take care of Mrs. Sarafiny by herself.

Anna answered the first question on the exam: "When should you brush your teeth?" Anna wrote, "After every meal or snack" even though she was positive that not even *teachers* brushed as often as that. Still, she knew it was the right answer.

Collin passed Anna another note from Bethie. It said:

> Anna,
> I don't know anything. But some people in jail and some people who die are crazy. Do you think that would happen to Mrs. Sarafiny?
>
> B.F.F.,
> Bethie

Anna wrote on the other side of the note:

Bethie,
I don't think Mrs. Sarafiny would ever hurt any-
body. But maybe she would get hurt herself.
                    B.F.F.,
                    Anna

Anna looked at the second test question. It said: "It's a good idea to bathe (how often?)_____." Personally, Anna felt once a week was more than enough. But she knew that in order to get a good grade, you really had to go crazy over personal hygiene. So she wrote, "Daily."

Then the note came back from Bethie. It said:

Anna,
What are we going to do?
                    B.F.F.,
                    Bethie

Anna thought, What are we going to do? I'm just not sure. Why don't they teach useful things in health, like how to help a crazy person?

Anna looked at the test paper with disgust. She just didn't feel like answering questions about brushing your teeth when she was worried about a

133

friend. Just then, she heard Miss Crystal say, "Everyone pass up your papers, please. Time is up."

But Anna wasn't finished with her test! She had answered only the first two questions! Anna raised her hand, "Miss Crystal, can I have a little more time with my test? I haven't finished it yet." Miss Crystal was kind and understanding. Surely she would give Anna as much time as she needed.

Miss Crystal walked to Anna's desk, her high heels tapping against the hard tile floor. She looked at Anna's paper. "Anna, you've answered only two questions," she said, "and I'm not surprised. I saw you daydreaming and passing notes to Bethie. Next time there's a test, maybe you'll remember to pay attention to your work." Miss Crystal picked up Anna's paper and took it to the front of the class, with all the rest.

Anna would fail her health test! She had never failed a test before. And worse! Now Miss Crystal thought she was a daydreamer. It was so unfair! All Anna was trying to do was help a friend, and now she was in trouble at school.

The day was terrible. It was cold and drizzly,

and there was no outside recess, so Anna couldn't find a way to talk to Bethie alone. She was worried about the health test and Miss Crystal's anger. She was worried about Mrs. Sarafiny. She was worried about Mom and Daddy finding out about Caroline and Mrs. Sarafiny. Anna's head ached and she felt very small.

After school, it was still raining and it smelled like wet worms. Bethie pulled up the hood on her rain parka. "Anna, I think we should go to Mrs. Sarafiny's," she said.

"I think so too." Anna didn't have a rain parka. She turned up the collar on her blue-jean jacket, but the rain made her face and hair wet. "We have to keep watching her to see if she gets worse."

"Yeah. And Anna—if she gets worse, maybe we have to get help."

"Probably. But I'm afraid to tell my parents, aren't you?" The drizzly rain dripped off Anna's lip. She caught the drips with her tongue.

"Yes. But we have to think about Mrs. Sarafiny. If she does get worse—if she really gets in trouble—we have to get help."

"Yes. If Mrs. Sarafiny's really in trouble, we'll get help."

Anna and Bethie took the school bus to Anna's house. Anna thought about changing her wet clothes, but she decided that would take too much time. Anna and Bethie walked toward Mrs. Sarafiny's. The rain had gotten worse. By the time they got there, Anna was soaking wet. Her socks were making little squidgy noises in her shoes. Water was running down her legs. Her skirt was dark and drippy. Her red hair hung in copper slashes against her forehead.

Before Anna knocked on Mrs. Sarafiny's door, she gave Bethie the Best Friends Handshake for luck. "Maybe she'll be fine today," Anna said. "Maybe the aluminum foil will be off, and she'll have some new food."

"And we can play canasta." Bethie's face was wet too. Drops of water ran in squiggly lines down her face.

"Yes." Anna knocked. Like the last time, it took a long time for Mrs. Sarafiny to open the door a crack.

"There's no one out here but me and Bethie," Anna offered. "I checked."

Mrs. Sarafiny scanned the air around Anna. Satisfied, she opened the door. "Hurry inside, girls. They're fast." Anna and Bethie hurried in.

Mrs. Sarafiny was wearing the shower cap again, lined with aluminum foil. The kitchen was still covered with it too. There were dark, heavy bags under Mrs. Sarafiny's eyes. It was cold in her house, and there weren't any lights on. Despite the cold, Mrs. Sarafiny was wearing the same summer dress she had worn for two days, and the same paper hospital slippers. Surely she must be cold. None of the cats were in the kitchen except for John, who was napping on the financial section. Mrs. Sarafiny and her cold, still house gave Anna a shivery feeling. Things didn't look very good.

Mrs. Sarafiny looked at Anna and Bethie. She said, "Are you hungry?"

Bethie said, "No. We had a big lunch at school." Outside, there was a whack of thunder. The storm was getting worse. Anna trembled from wet and cold and worry.

"You must be hungry," Mrs. Sarafiny insisted. "I'm hungry. Let's have a TV dinner!"

"Oh!" Anna said. Since Bethie and Anna hadn't brought Mrs. Sarafiny TV dinners, it meant she must have gone shopping herself. That was a good sign! "That would be great, Mrs. Sarafiny!"

Anna and Bethie sat at the kitchen table with John and watched, with growing surprise, as Mrs. Sarafiny unplugged the small television set from the wall. They watched as she turned on the oven and put the television inside.

"What are you doing?" Anna asked.

"Why, making a TV dinner, of course!" said Mrs. Sarafiny. She laughed merrily and slapped her thigh with her hand. "Isn't it a great idea?" Mrs. Sarafiny pulled a chair up to the glass oven door and turned on the light inside.

"I don't know how long this will take," Mrs. Sarafiny told Bethie. "I've never made a TV dinner before."

Anna stood up. "Mrs. Sarafiny, I think you'd better turn off the oven. I'm afraid the television will explode or something."

"Nonsense." Mrs. Sarafiny chuckled. "These things are meant to cook. That's why they're called TV dinners. Have you ever heard of a cold TV dinner?"

Now Anna knew the truth. Mrs. Sarafiny *could* get hurt. Her craziness was real, and her problem was too big for Bethie and her to handle by

themselves. Anna looked at Bethie. Bethie's eyes said what Anna knew: Let's get out of here. Let's get help. No matter how much trouble it made for Anna at home, it was clear that she had to get help for her friend. Anna said, "I just remembered something, Mrs. Sarafiny. I have to go home for a few minutes."

"Me too," said Bethie.

Anna tried one more time. "Please turn off the oven, Mrs. Sarafiny. I'm really afraid the television will blow up."

"Don't be silly! Who ever heard of an exploding TV dinner?" Mrs. Sarafiny said.

Anna stood still for a minute, afraid to leave Mrs. Sarafiny with the cooking TV and afraid to stay. Then Anna rushed to her friend and hugged her. "Don't worry, Mrs. Sarafiny. Everything will be okay." But Anna wondered if it would.

When Anna opened the door, it seemed as if she had been hit by a wall of water. Anna and Bethie ran. Their shoes sunk into the mud, and small waves of water arched away from their feet.

"Where should we go for help?" Bethie shouted. Bethie's words were muffled by the noise of the storm, and Anna could hardly hear her.

"Home," Anna screamed back. Home was safe and dry. There were people who loved her, people who could help. But would Mom and Daddy be angry that she hadn't told them about Caroline and Mrs. Sarafiny? Would they be so angry that they would not help? Anna thought of sitting on Mom's lap, cozy and snug while watching the storm. She thought of Daddy, his long arms wrapped around her. Mom always said Anna could tell her anything. Daddy always said he was there to help. Well, this was the real test, wasn't it? Would Mom and Daddy be true to their word? Would they listen to Anna and think about helping instead of scolding? In the mean-time, what would happen to Mrs. Sarafiny? Would the television explode? Would the oven start a fire? Would Mrs. Sarafiny be trapped in a burning house?

Anna and Bethie ran. Thunder clapped and lightning exploded in the sky. Anna had never been outside in a storm this bad. It seemed as though the waves from Green Bay had escaped the shores and were pouring on top of Anna and Bethie. The friends slogged through the storm, clinging to each other.

At last, there was Anna's gray house. Anna flung open the door and they ran inside, spraying drops of water. Daddy was at the kitchen table and Mom was beside him. A glass lamp glowed soft and yellow over their heads. Kimberly was at music lessons, Anna remembered. She sighed. She and Bethie had taken care of things by themselves for so long that she was tired, inside and out. Anna wanted Mom and Daddy to hold her now. She wanted them to take care of Mrs. Sarafiny, and she wanted them to take care of her.

"Mom. Daddy," Anna said.

Mom and Daddy looked up. They saw Bethie's and Anna's wet, worried faces. "Anna, Bethie," Daddy said, blinking.

"What's the problem?" Mom asked.

9

HELP

Anna drew in a big breath. She didn't know where to start. But somehow she had to make sense, and make sense quickly. "I just came from Mrs. Sarafiny's house—"

Mom jumped in. "Mrs. Sarafiny? Anna, you aren't supposed to—"

But Daddy interrupted. "Let Anna talk. There's some kind of trouble."

"Yes! That's what it is. Big trouble. Mrs. Sarafiny's crazy. She thinks the Martians are after her, and she's covered her kitchen in aluminum foil to protect her from rays." Anna talked quickly, and the words tumbled over themselves. "She's all alone and she put a TV in the oven because she thinks it's a TV dinner and the TV might start on fire and she might get hurt and maybe the cats will be hurt too. She has seven cats."

Mom asked, "Is the TV cooking in the oven right now?"

Bethie said, "Yes."

"And there's nobody with Mrs. Sarafiny?" Daddy asked.

"No," Anna said.

Daddy hurried to the phone. He dialed and said, "Sheriff? This is Paul Skoggen. This is an emergency. There's a woman near Prairie View Court—Mrs. Sarafiny—who's been acting very strangely. She just put a TV in the oven. There could be a fire or an explosion."

There was silence from Daddy's end while the sheriff talked. Then he said, "My daughter Anna knows her." A quick silence. Then Daddy said, "Yes. That's a good idea. It's the house on Cherrywood Hill."

Daddy walked quickly to Bethie and Anna.

"The sheriff said Mrs. Sarafiny may have to be hospitalized. He's going to her house now, along with someone from the Mental Health Center. He'll call later and tell us what happened."

"I want to go along," Anna said.

"Me too," said Bethie.

"Absolutely not," Mom said. "It could be dangerous. There might be a fire."

"If there's a fire, I'll stay out of the house. But Mrs. Sarafiny's afraid of Martians. She's *really* afraid. She'll never let the sheriff in her house because she doesn't know him."

"Anna and I are her friends. She'd let us in," Bethie said.

Mom and Daddy were quiet for a few seconds. Then Mom said, "The girls are right. Mrs. Sarafiny will trust them. Maybe they should go along."

"Yes," Daddy agreed. "I'll take them."

"I'll stay home and wait for Kimberly. She's still at her music lessons. I'll also need to make some phone calls. If Mrs. Sarafiny has to go to a hospital, we'll have to find someone to take care of her cats for a while."

"Good thinking, Helen," Daddy said.

145

Inside the car, Anna thought: Please be all right, Mrs. Sarafiny. Please be all right.

When they got to Mrs. Sarafiny's, two cars were already in the driveway. One of them was the sheriff's squad car. A man in a plastic-covered sheriff's hat and a woman in a raincoat were trying to talk to Mrs. Sarafiny through the door. The door was chained shut.

"Go away," Mrs. Sarafiny shouted through the small opening. "I know who you are, and I'm not letting you in. Do you think I was born yesterday?" Then she slammed the door shut.

The sheriff had a fire extinguisher. He said to the woman, "We're going to have to break in."

"That would really frighten her. It would be much better if she let us in."

"Sheriff!" Anna called.

The sheriff turned around as Anna and Bethie rushed toward him. "We're Mrs. Sarafiny's friends," Bethie said.

"I think we can get her to open the door," Anna said. Before the sheriff could say "No," Anna knocked on the door. "Mrs. Sarafiny! It's me, Anna."

"And Bethie."

146

"Remember? We said we'd come back."

Mrs. Sarafiny opened the door again. It was still chained. "Anna and Bethie, watch out! Those are the Martians on the porch!"

"No they're not, Mrs. Sarafiny," Bethie said. "It's the sheriff and a hospital lady."

Anna looked at the sheriff's plastic-covered hat. "See the sheriff's hat? It's covered—like yours. If he was a Martian, he wouldn't have a covered hat. And that thing he's carrying"— Anna nodded at the fire extinguisher—"is for protection."

Mrs. Sarafiny undid the chain and opened the door. "All right," she said. "Come in."

Inside, the kitchen was filled with black smoke that stung Anna's eyes. There were so many big people in front of her that Anna couldn't see anything else.

"Stay back," the sheriff said. He pushed through the smoke. Anna heard a loud whooshing noise. She knew it was the fire extinguisher. The TV, the oven—something!—must be on fire. Then the sheriff opened the windows. As the smoke in the kitchen cleared, Anna could see Mrs. Sarafiny, sitting in front of the oven. She looked confused and she was talking softly to herself. John, the financial cat, was on her lap. Three of the cats were slunk low and wild-eyed in the corner.

"Who are you?" Mrs. Sarafiny asked the sheriff.

"I'm Sheriff Goetz," he said. "You know Bethie and Anna. This is Anna's dad and another friend, Dr. Holmes. We're here to help you, Mrs. Sarafiny."

Dr. Holmes began to talk. "Mrs. Sarafiny, your house isn't safe for you right now. We want to take you to a safe place." Dr. Holmes talked smoothly, softly, like Mom did when she kissed Anna good-night.

"No," Mrs. Sarafiny said. She spoke so softly it was hard to hear her. "I'm staying here."

"Mrs. Sarafiny, this house isn't safe for you. Look what happened with the TV in the oven."

Mrs. Sarafiny stuck out her chin. "That was because of the Martians. They're responsible for the fire." Mrs. Sarafiny looked around the room. "Can't you see them? They're laughing at us now."

Dr. Holmes looked carefully around the house. She even opened a few cupboards. "No, I don't see them now. But I know of a place that's safe."

148

"But the Martians are everywhere," Mrs. Sarafiny said. "Look what they did to my TV dinner! No place is safe. Where do you want to take me, anyway?"

"To a hospital where we can take care of you," Dr. Holmes said.

Anna said, "Dr. Holmes will take you to a place where you won't get hurt."

Mrs. Sarafiny sank deeply into her chair. "I'm so tired. And I've always liked hospitals. Nice and clean." She looked at Bethie and Anna. "Do you girls think it will be okay?"

Anna and Bethie hugged Mrs. Sarafiny. They pressed into her and Bethie said, "It will be okay."

"Yes," Anna said.

Mrs. Sarafiny got up out of her chair. Suddenly, she looked very young to Anna, instead of very old. Her face was clear and smooth. "All right then."

The sheriff took Mrs. Sarafiny's arm. "Believe me, the hospital is a safe place. It's bright and cheery. There are lots of windows and some plants, and maybe you'll meet new friends. Dr. Holmes will take good care of you."

Suddenly Mrs. Sarafiny pulled back. She looked alarmed. "But what about the kitties? The Martians will get them here."

"Mom is going to find someone to take care of the kitties," Anna said. But she was also worried. What would Mrs. Sarafiny do without her wonderful cats? She would be so lonely without them! Wouldn't she get better if she had one or two cats with her?

"Dr. Holmes," Anna began. "Is there a hospital rule against bringing an animal along?"

"Not really, Anna," Dr. Holmes said. "In fact, we've been thinking about getting a cat at the center anyway. Some studies say that people get better when they have an animal around."

"Can the animals be Caroline and John?"

The whole group was silent for several minutes. Anna's question hung in the air like the remaining smoke.

"Yes," Dr. Holmes said finally.

Anna walked toward the kitties huddled in the corner. She picked up Caroline. Caroline's fur was sticking out like Anna's cowlick. Her eyes were big and round. Anna talked softly to Caroline, the way Dr. Holmes talked to Mrs. Sarafiny. It was a taking-care-of voice. "Caroline, you go along with Mrs. Sarafiny. You'll go to a cheery place, a place where there will be lots of people to play with you."

It seemed like a perfect circle. Mrs. Sarafiny had rescued Anna and Caroline. Now Caroline and Anna were rescuing Mrs. Sarafiny. "Here you are," Anna said, placing Caroline gently in Mrs. Sarafiny's arms, where she nestled beside John. "I'll visit you in the hospital, Mrs. Sarafiny. I promise."

"Yes. That would be nice. It's safe there, Anna."

Dr. Holmes said, "Mrs. Sarafiny, you're lucky to have such good friends." Then she said to Bethie and Anna, "We'll probably give Mrs. Sarafiny some medicine that will help her think more clearly. In a few days, she should feel a lot better."

"And we can visit her?" asked Anna.

"Yes, I think she'd really like to see you both."

The sheriff and Dr. Holmes led Mrs. Sarafiny, still carrying John and Caroline, to the squad car. Mrs. Sarafiny turned toward Bethie and Anna. As the rain fell on her, she touched her fingertips to

151

her lips. She threw them a kiss and waved good-bye to Bethie and Anna.

Daddy drove to Bethie's to drop her off. Solemnly, silently, Bethie got out of the car and waved good-bye to Anna. Anna began to shake. She was so wet! She was so cold and tired! Dr. Holmes seemed to think Mrs. Sarafiny would be better in a few days. Anna hoped it was true! As Daddy drove home, Anna watched the sturdy windshield wipers wipe away the waves of rain.

The blue car pulled up in the driveway, and Anna saw the porch light blink on and off. That was the family's signal. It meant "Welcome home." As soon as Daddy and Anna came in, Mom ran up to them. "Is everything okay?"

"Yes," Daddy said. Mrs. Sarafiny's on her way to the Mental Health Center. They'll take care of her—give her medication, talk to her—and they think she'll be better soon."

Mom sighed with relief. "Oh, that's wonderful!"

"And I'm going to visit her," Anna reminded Daddy.

"Yes. Dr. Holmes said it would be okay."

"Now Anna, you're wet and shaking. Put on

your robe and slippers and come downstairs for a family cuddle. We won't have dinner until Kimberly's home from music lessons."

Slowly, Anna walked upstairs. Normally she ran up, sometimes taking the steps two at a time, but now she was like a doll with no bones. It took a long time for Anna to peel her clothes off. She went to the bathroom and dried herself off with a big towel. Anna slid into her quilted robe. It felt wonderful against her pale, goose-bumpy skin. Anna's legs were wobbly and her skin hurt as she stepped slowly down the stairs, holding on to the railing.

Mom rushed toward Anna, picked her up, and carried her to the couch, where Daddy was waiting. Anna bent over Mom's left shoulder. Gently, Mom lowered Anna onto the couch and held her tightly.

Anna watched the storm from Mom's arms. She watched the sky crackle with lightning. She watched the water pour down the windows in small rivers. The water caught a feather, maybe from a sea gull, and now it was washing it away, pushing it down the window. Anna remembered that once, when she was swimming, she'd gotten into a strong current. The current had pulled Anna and dragged her along. Anna had kicked and stroked to get out of the current, but she couldn't. She had felt weak, as if she had no muscles. But somehow Anna had been able to grab on to the root of a tree. She had pulled herself out. But she had felt terribly small and helpless after that, because she knew that the current was so much stronger than she was.

"Daddy," Anna said, in a faraway voice, "will Mrs. Sarafiny be all right?"

"Yes," he said. "The medicine and doctors will help."

And now, an even harder question. Anna closed her eyes to ask it. "Are you and Mom going to get a divorce?"

Daddy answered quickly. "Why of course not, Anna! Whatever made you ask such a thing?"

"Because sometimes you fight."

Mom said, "Do you and Kimberly fight?"

Anna opened her eyes. "Yes."

"And how about you and Bethie?" Daddy asked.

"Not a lot, but sometimes."

Mom smiled. "I really love Daddy, Anna, but

sometimes I get angry with him." She shrugged. "So sometimes we fight."

"Fighting doesn't mean divorce, Anna," Daddy said. "It just means we disagree." Then Daddy wrapped his arms around Mom and Anna together. It was Anna's favorite kind of hug. She called it an "Anna sandwich." Inside the sandwich, Anna felt safe and snug. She knew that together, the people in the hug were stronger than the current.

10

SUNSHINE
AND CAROLINE

Hospitals were exciting places. Anna liked the drama of them—life and death, blood and moaning, babies and good news. She liked the soothing way doctors and nurses talked and the fast, silent way they walked, almost as if they had wheels instead of legs. She liked the fact that they could help people get better. But what if Mrs. Sarafiny didn't get better? What if she could never come home and had to stay in the hospital forever? The thought of that made Anna's stomach churn. She wanted Mrs. Sarafiny to be happy and live in her own house again.

Anna worried about that all the way to the Mental Health Center. It had been five days since she'd seen Mrs. Sarafiny. What would she be like now? Outside, the hospital looked nice enough. There was a playground. There were good climbing trees and cheerful pots of rust-colored flowers at the door. Mom opened the door, and Anna and Bethie walked in behind her.

"May I help you?" asked the receptionist, who had a pencil behind her ear and glasses hanging from a string around her neck. She was sitting behind a large desk.

"We're here to see Mrs. Sarafiny," Mom explained.

The receptionist smiled. Anna noticed that the bottom part of one of her teeth was tipped in gold. It looked pretty, like mouth jewelry. "Dr. Holmes said you'd be coming. Mrs. Sarafiny is on Three-West. Take the elevator to your right."

Anna let Mom lead the way to the elevator and she let her punch the button for the third floor. Normally, Anna liked to lead and she *always* liked to punch the elevator buttons. But today she felt a little shy.

Ding! The elevator doors opened. Anna and Bethie walked with their hands stiffly at their sides. Anna was aware that her knee sock had drooped down to her ankle and was scrunching inside her shoe. There was a sock lump in her shoe now, but she didn't want to bend over to pull up her sock. She could only stare straight ahead at the big door that said "3-West." The top of the door had a small window with criss-crossed wires. The wires, Anna thought, look like the kind you would have in a prison, not a hospital.

Mom rang a buzzer at the door and a voice echoed through a speaker. "May I help you?" Speakers and wired windows and buzzers made Anna nervous.

"This is Mrs. Skoggen," Mom said. "We're here to see Mrs. Sarafiny."

"Dr. Holmes will be right with you," the voice said brightly.

Very soon Dr. Holmes opened the door. Anna was surprised to find she wasn't wearing regular hospital clothes. She didn't have on a white coat. She wore a silky blouse and green swirly skirt— just the kind Anna liked—and black heels with bows on them. "Oh, Anna and Bethie! Mrs.

Sarafiny has been asking about you. She'll be so happy you're here." Dr. Holmes pumped Anna's and Bethie's hands enthusiastically.

Then Dr. Holmes said, "You must be Anna's mother!"

"Yes," Mom said, smiling.

"Come this way, everybody." Dr. Holmes walked briskly along the tan carpeting. She led the way to a large room. One whole wall was windows—big, bright ones. The windows faced Green Bay. Anna thought Lake Michigan had never looked more beautiful. The blues and greens swirled over each other and the sea gulls dove merrily above. It must be nice, Anna thought, for a sad person to look at something so happy. There were several tables in the room, one with people playing cards. A TV was on in a corner. There were books on the shelves and magazines on the tables, and there were colorful plants all over. This is a nice place, Anna thought. Mrs. Sarafiny must like it.

And then she saw her, sitting in a purple chair. Mrs. Sarafiny was facing the window, so Anna couldn't see her face. But she recognized her white, frizzy hair and the hat made out of bread wrappers.

Anna and Bethie ran to their friend. "Mrs. Sarafiny," Bethie cried.

Mrs. Sarafiny turned. "Anna! Bethie!" Mrs. Sarafiny's face looked very cheerful as Anna and Bethie rushed over to her and put their arms around her. Mrs. Sarafiny was all right! Anna could see it in her face. Then she felt something squirm beneath her. A tiny head poked out of the tangle of arms. It was Caroline! Anna picked her up.

"Caroline!" She kissed the kitten on the nose, and Caroline ran her sand-papery tongue across Anna's chin. "Do you like it here, Caroline?"

"You bet your booties," said a man with spiky gray hair who was sitting close by. "She's a little princess, that one."

"This is my friend," Mrs. Sarafiny said. "Tom."

Tom winked. "Violet and I share a love of jelly doughnuts and cats, don't we, Vi?" John was stretched out on Tom's lap, his gray head resting on Tom's book, *Making Big Bucks on Little Stock Tips.*

Mrs. Sarafiny smiled shyly. "Tom loves Caroline and John. They're my cats, so I get to hold them when I want to. But I let Tom have a turn now and then."

"I'll see you later, Vi. Want me to set up canasta?" Tom asked.

"Just as long as you don't stack the deck, you stinker," Mrs. Sarafiny said, laughing. Then she whispered, cupping her hand, to Anna and Bethie, "Never trust anybody at cards."

Dr. Holmes said, "Bringing Caroline and John here was a great idea, Anna. Everyone here loves the cats. They're so playful and lovable that they're really helping people get better."

Anna grinned. She was happy she'd thought of the cats too. She must have a way with helping people. Maybe it was a sign, she thought, that she was going to be a doctor. And the fact that she'd be able to wear swirly skirts instead of stiff white clothes was a good sign too. Anna wondered if she could be a doctor *and* a famous author.

Mrs. Sarafiny looked at Mom. "Who are you?"

"I'm Helen Skoggen, Anna's mother."

Mrs. Sarafiny stuck out her hand. "Pleased to

meetcha, Helen. A mother of Anna's is a friend of mine." Mrs. Sarafiny laughed at her little joke.

"There's coffee over there," Dr. Holmes said to Mom. "Help yourself." Dr. Holmes looked at her watch, a green one with black stripes. "I've got to take care of some things. But I'll be back in a little bit." Then she walked away, her skirt swirling around her legs.

As Mom walked to the corner for coffee, Mrs. Sarafiny began to talk with a serious face. "Have you seen my cats? Are they all right? Are they getting enough to eat? They need plenty of fresh water, you know, and Jenny hates it when the kitty litter gets dirty."

"The cats are fine, Mrs. Sarafiny," Bethie said, nodding.

"Bethie and I take turns. We go to your house every day and give the cats fresh food and water," Anna said.

"Well, now, you have to change their litter. Cats are very clean animals."

"We do!" Bethie said. It was gross to clean the cat litter, and both girls held their noses when they did it. But they kept the litter clean because of Mrs. Sarafiny and the cats.

"Do you play with them? They're used to lots of attention, you know, and they'd be very sad without someone to handle them and love them." Mrs. Sarafiny was about to cry.

Anna hugged her friend again. "I love to do that, Mrs. Sarafiny. Since I can't have cats of my own, I'm happy to play with yours."

Mrs. Sarafiny wiped her eyes and settled back into her chair, satisfied. The light from the sunny window made her glow. Just then, Dr. Holmes arrived with soda and jelly doughnuts on a blue plastic tray. "I thought your guests might like a little snack," she said, passing out drinks and doughnuts to Bethie, Anna, and Mrs. Sarafiny. Anna took a sip of the soda. It was cold and icy, just the way she liked it.

"I'll leave you with your guests again, Violet. I'd like to talk with Anna's mother." Dr. Holmes poured herself a cup of coffee and sat down with Mom. Anna really wanted to know what they were talking about. Whenever grown-ups had coffee without kids, Anna knew they were having an Important Talk. But she was convinced she'd get Mom to tell about it later.

Anna watched Tom shuffle a deck of cards. She

admired the way the cards, moving in a swift arc, slid into place in Tom's hands. He looked like a magician. Tom glanced at Anna and Bethie. "Do these ladies know how to play?" he asked Mrs. Sarafiny.

"Of course," said Mrs. Sarafiny. "I taught them all I know."

"Good," said Tom. "Then I can beat the socks off them." He slid his chair in with his feet, and was right between Bethie and Mrs. Sarafiny. He began to deal the cards, but Mrs. Sarafiny gently slapped his hand. "What's this? Dealing without a cut?" Laughing, Mrs. Sarafiny divided the deck in two and put the bottom half on top. Then she said to the girls, "Number one rule: Always cut the deck. Number two rule: Never trust anyone at cards."

When Tom smiled, Anna knew. Tom was Mrs. Sarafiny's friend. He liked to kid around with her. He *liked* her. Anna could see that Mrs. Sarafiny was happier, less confused. This hospital was a nice place, and it was making her better. But Anna was still worried. Would Mrs. Sarafiny have to stay here forever? Would she be healthy in the hospital, and then get sick at home?

The card game was a riot. There was a little pile of silver coins on the table, because they played for nickels. Mrs. Sarafiny called the pile "the kitty." That was especially funny, because John sat on the table and kept a close eye on the coins as they passed from hand to hand.

Later, they counted their money. "I won fifteen cents!" whooped Mrs. Sarafiny, jiggling the coins around in her hand.

"Well, dad-burn it," said Tom. "I lost a quarter." Tom slapped the table with the palm of his hand, but his eyes were twinkling. He wasn't really angry.

Mrs. Sarafiny took her brightly colored Manzanillo bag and pulled out a coin purse. She tossed the coins in and snapped it shut. "There's nothing I like more than winning at canasta, though maybe I should have made it easier on Tom," she said to Anna, winking. "It was too easy—like taking candy from a baby."

Bethie and Anna had each won a nickel. Anna would be happy to refill her nearly empty jar. It was a beginning.

Mom and Dr. Holmes walked up. Mom said, "Anna and Bethie, I'm afraid it's time to leave."

167

Anna was ready. It was nice visiting her friend, but Anna felt squirmy inside. She wanted to ride bikes with Bethie. Anna and Bethie hugged Mrs. Sarafiny.

"Well, it sure was the cat's pajamas seeing you two again," said Mrs. Sarafiny, in the middle of a Mrs. Sarafiny sandwich.

Anna kissed Mrs. Sarafiny's freckled cheek. "Yes. We'll come again."

"We promise," said Bethie.

On the way home, Mom said, "Anna and Bethie, your visit really cheered up Mrs. Sarafiny. You really are good friends to her. I'm proud of both of you."

"Thanks, Mrs. Skoggen," Bethie said politely.

Anna waited in silence for a few minutes. Maybe Mom would just tell her what Dr. Holmes had said. When she didn't, Anna said, "Mom, what were you and Dr. Holmes talking about?"

"When?" asked Mom.

"You know . . . when you were having coffee. When we were playing cards."

"Well, Dr. Holmes told me about Mrs. Sarafiny's progress."

Honestly! Did Anna have to pull everything

out of her mother, one sentence at a time? "Please, Mom. Tell us everything she said. We were grown-up enough to help Mrs. Sarafiny. We're grown-up enough to understand her sickness."

Mom nodded. "You're right, Anna. Sometimes I forget how grown-up you really are. Mrs. Sarafiny has paranoid schizophrenia. She has responded very well to medicine, so Dr. Holmes is quite certain she'll be fine. Probably she'll be able to go home in a week or so."

"Then what?" asked Bethie. "How will they know she'll be all right? How do they know she won't get sick again?"

"She'll continue to take medicine for a while," Mom explained. "And she'll come back to the hospital as an outpatient."

"What?!" asked Anna. "A patient is either *in* the hospital or *out* of it. How can you be an outpatient?"

"Mrs. Sarafiny will live at home—the same as always. But she'll come to the hospital for a visit twice a week. Once, she'll come for lunch. There will be other people there, and they'll have a nice time together. The other time she'll come for

169

some kind of activity—a party, maybe, or exercises or a craft project—always with other people."

"Like Tom?" Anna asked.

"Yes, I'm sure Tom will be there too," Mom said.

"That sounds nice," said Bethie. "It's sort of like day camp."

"Yes. Maybe Mrs. Sarafiny can teach the other outpatients how to make hats out of bread wrappers," Anna said.

"Anyway, Dr. Holmes will keep an eye on Mrs. Sarafiny when she visits. If she starts acting sick again, they'll give her a little more medicine until she's okay."

Anna was satisfied. She leaned her red head against the seat of the car, just at the spot where her cowlick stuck out. She sighed deeply. The sunshine and Caroline and Mrs. Sarafiny and her new nickel filled her with happiness. She wriggled her toes against the tip of her too-small sneakers and pulled her knee sock up.

FIC
JOO

Joosse, Barbara M.

Anna and the cat lady.